THE HOUSEWIFE ASSASSIN'S MANNERS, MISSILES, AND MAYHEM

The Housewife Assassin Series
Book 22

JOSIE BROWN

A BOOK BY

SIGNAL PRESS

ONE OF MANY GREAT SIGNAL PRESS BOOKS

San Francisco, CA

Library of Congress Cataloging-in-Publication Data is available upon request

Cover Design by Andrew Brown, ClickTwiceDesign.com

Trade Paperback ISBN: 978-1-970093-25-4

Hardcover ISBN: 978-1-970093-45-2

V110722

"This is a super sexy and fun read that you shouldn't miss! A kick ass woman that can literally kick ass as well as cook and clean. Donna gives a whole new meaning to "taking out the trash."
—Mary Jacobs, *Book Hounds Reviews*

"The Housewife Assassin's Handbook by Josie Brown is a fun, sexy and intriguing mystery. Donna Stone is a great heroine—housewives can lead all sorts of double lives, but as an assassin? Who would have seen that one coming? It's a fast-paced read, the gadgets are awesome, and I could just picture Donna fighting off Russian gangsters and skin-heads all the while having a pie at home cooling on the windowsill. As a housewife myself, this book was a fantastic escape that had me dreaming "if only" the whole way through. The book doesn't take itself too seriously, which makes for the perfect combination of mystery and humour."
—*Curled Up with a Good Book and a Cup of Tea*

"*The Housewife Assassin's Handbook* is a hilarious, laugh-out-loud read. Donna is a fantastic character–practical, witty, and kick-ass tough. There's plenty of action–both in and out of the bedroom… I especially love the housekeeping tips at the start of each chapter–each with its own deadly twist! This book is perfect for relaxing in the bath with after a long day. I can't wait to read the next in the series. Highly Recommended!"

—CrimeThrillerGirl.com

"This was an addictive read–gritty but funny at the same time. I ended up reading it in just one evening and couldn't go to sleep until I knew what the outcome would be! It was action-packed and humorous from the start, and that continued throughout, I was pleased to discover that this is the first of a series and look forward to getting my hands on Book Two so I can see where life takes Donna and her family next!"

—Me, My Books, and I

"The two halves of Donna's life make sense. As you follow her story, there's no point where you think of her as "Assassin Donna" vs. "Mummy Donna', her attitude to life is even throughout. I really like how well this is done. And as for Jack. I'll have one of those, please?"

—The Northern Witch's Book Blog

Novels in The Housewife Assassin Series

The Housewife Assassin's Handbook

(Book 1)

The Housewife Assassin's Guide to Gracious Killing

(Book 2)

The Housewife Assassin's Killer Christmas Tips

(Book 3)

The Housewife Assassin's Relationship Survival Guide

(Book 4)

The Housewife Assassin's Vacation to Die For

(Book 5)

The Housewife Assassin's Recipes for Disaster

(Book 6)

The Housewife Assassin's Hollywood Scream Play

(Book 7)

The Housewife Assassin's Killer App

(Book 8)

The Housewife Assassin's Hostage Hosting Tips

(Book 9)

The Housewife Assassin's Garden of Deadly Delights

(Book 10)

The Housewife Assassin's Tips for

Grin and Bear It

IT'S A JUNGLE OUT THERE—

Beyond the comfort of your serene home.

Since there are no guarantees that those you meet beyond your picket fence will have been raised with the grace, courage, and wit you embody, plan to leave prepared for any emergency, including:

*1: **A first aid kit!** Think your Fendi Baguette is complete with your favorite lipstick and embroidered hankies? Wrong! Burn cream, aspirin, an instant cold compress, various sizes of adhesive bandages, and wound closure strips aren't fashionable, but they may save a life.*

*2: **Self-defense weapon.** A pocketknife, Mace, or 22 caliber mini revolver will fit easily into your purse. Even that travel-size Poo-Pouri spray will come in handy when spritzed in your assailant's eye.*

*3: **A quick getaway plan.** Don't count on your GPS to guide you—especially if enemy territory may be monitored for* *unauthorized intruders. In fact, best lose the phone on some unsuspecting pedestrian going in the opposite direction so that your detainers lose your trail. Instead, go old school and carry a map of the territory you've already memorized for the ideal escape route and rendezvous point with your rescue squad. And so they can find you where X marks the spot, carry a flare gun.*

(It will also make your point to any jerk who gets touchy-feely in an elevator.)

HELLO DARKNESS, MY OLD FRIEND...

There is no moonlight tonight. Like Harry Potter's invisible cloak, the inky night shrouds my daughter, Mary, and me from prying eyes.

Not that any are about. Sadly, we're in the last few days of our mother-daughter two-week getaway, deep in the seven-hundred-acre Cleveland National Forest. We're four hours south and east of our home in Hilldale, California, and twelve miles from the nearest town: Mesa Grande.

Mary and I have hunkered down in a thicket of pines next to a small lake fed by several creeks still flowing in late May from snow runoff. A fallen tree sheared of its branches gives us cover. Night vision goggles allow us to scan the lake's banks for Mary's prey: deer, which she must kill with a compound bow.

From the side of her mouth, Mary hisses: "Of all the things I've done these past couple of weeks, who knew my very last assignment would be killing *Bambi*!"

"The deer population in this park has exploded, so

don't feel guilty. Because this trip is to give you a reality check on whether you really want to get into the family business—diplomatic intelligence—I took advantage of it being deer season and secured a hunting license and two deer tags for you. The timing is perfect since you'll be gone the rest of the summer."

Mary snickers. "I now easily hit bullseyes in target practice. And by the way, there are very few deer inside embassies."

"But there *are* a hell of a lot of assassins. So, as you learned in Girl Scouts, be prepared. In this case, that means knowing how to exterminate based on the situation and the weapon at your disposal." I tap the bow in her hands. "Tell you what: if your first kill shot is clean, we'll forego the second. Okay?"

"Yeah, okay." She sighs. "Well, I guess it's better than using a rifle. Or my Sig Sauer."

I shake my head. "Way too easy. Hey, you're lucky I don't want you to stun it or trap it and then cut its throat. Or worse yet, blow it to bits with a land mine."

"You know, any other mom would have taken her daughter for a spa weekend," Mary mutters.

"All the more reason you've impressed me by sticking it out. You've learned vital survival skills these two weeks. Not one task I've thrown at you has phased you. And don't forget: you beat me twice at hand-to-hand combat."

"After being bested by you, what, the first hundred times?" Mary reminds me.

"And you can now live off the land," I point out. "You've even improved on my rabbit stew, not to mention you've identified seven deadly poisons and now know how to use them effectively."

"I still have nightmares about killing those rats," she counters.

"Next time, we won't secure our tent against them, and then let's see how you feel about the critters. As for other new covert intelligence skills, you can now add Morse code to your repertoire—"

"Which I use in my sleep, apparently," Mary grouses. "Sorry I woke you those first few nights."

"No problem, honey," I assure her. "Though the message was a bit perplexing—something about waterboarding me...which brings up another of your great new skills! You can hold your breath for almost three minutes underwater."

"That's only because you threatened to hold my head beneath the surface if I didn't reach two and a half minutes." Mary rolls her eyes.

"Persistence, darling, is the key to success." I'm joking, but she isn't laughing. I shrug. "Hey, the Golden Door is just an hour or two away. If you say, 'let's go,' no harm, no foul. But since you insist this is a life you want, you can't be afraid to defend yourself, even if it means killing. Even if you presume the target to be non-threatening."

"To be honest, learning to rappel up the cliff had me thinking twice about choosing this over lifeguarding at the Hilldale Swim & Racquet Center."

I snicker at that—

Only to have Mary put her hand over my mouth. She shifts her gaze to the lake's muddy banks, where a ten-point Columbian black-tailed buck now stands, still and silent, not fifty yards from us. His nose quivers as he sniffs the air. A moment later, he's grazing.

Confidently, Mary eases her palm away from me onto the bow she holds in her other hand. She's using a 70-weight medium-cam Punisher with a 25-inch bolt and titanium broadhead. I watch as Mary stares into her laser rangefinder, calculating the distance between her and her prey: 150 feet. She adjusts the bow's eccentricities for maximum extension. Her slight nod informs me that the broadhead is now aligned with the deer for the kill shot: the unobstructed lower third of its chest cavity can be seen diagonally from her point of view.

The arrow's hiss is no more than a whisper. And yet, the buck, attuned to it, looks up at that moment. Even so, he can't move quickly enough before the sharp metal tip of the bolt pierces him. With a grunt and a thud, he flops to the ground.

As she rises, Mary sighs, "I know, I know. I've got to carry it out of here to our campsite, then cut it up for meat. *Yuck*! I'm seriously considering veganism." She ambles toward the buck. When she reaches it, she drops her bow and quiver, then crouches down and grabs zip ties from her back pocket—

Totally forgetting one of my rock-solid rules: *surveil the area first.*

She doesn't see the brown bear and two cubs swimming up to shore. The scent of the downed buck caught their attention. Why trawl for fish when a venison dinner waits onshore?

The cubs are too enthralled by the smell of meat to notice Mary, but Mama sees her. Fearing for her cubs, she thrashes her way through the marshes.

The cubs flee in confusion as Mary looks up, frozen in fear.

I'm now running fast and stretched to my fullest height, hands waving crazily over my head, bellowing blasphemies at Mama Bear.

Mary follows my lead, rising tall and shouting guttural curses as if possessed. And unlike me, she has the where-withal to pull out her canister of bear spray from her back holster.

Mama snarls and grunts. The non-lethal shot leaves her pawing at her face and desperate to fill her lungs. She has no choice but to follow her twins' retreat.

Mary collapses against a tree. "Wow, Mom! She—*she would have killed me!*"

"In her mind you were a threat to her cubs," I explain. "Had you stood up immediately, snared, then backed off slowly, I think the dead deer would have distracted them. Remember: they're after food. They don't mind foraging some other animal's carrion—even ours."

"Then let's leave it for them. I'm not into venison anyway."

"Agreed. The bears will appreciate it more than us anyway. They're too skinny for this time of year."

Mary is shivering. This up-close-and-personal look at Mother Nature has left her shaken, but at least she has a rational understanding of why the bear reacted, and what if she's ever caught in this situation again.

In time, she walks over to the dead buck. By putting her foot against its chest, Mary has the leverage to yank out the bolt. As she picks up her quiver, her face takes on a quizzical look. "Are bears being hunted now, too?"

"Not until August. Only seventeen hundred can be killed, and only one per hunter." I don't want to add that had it been a black bear—even more common now in these parts—the stand tall-and-scream ploy would not have worked.

We've walked just a few yards when we hear gunfire coming from behind us. In unison, we stop in our tracks and stare at each other.

"I thought you said it wasn't bear season," Mary says.

"It's not," I insist.

"Do you think it was another hunter killing a deer?"

"Only bows allowed," I remind her.

We hear a noise coming our way through the thicket: as if something is being dragged. A moment later, a man—wearing camo head to toe—comes into view. Before he glances our way, I duck beneath a fallen tree, but I can watch him through its branches.

Mary isn't so quick. She's staring at his catch: a lifeless, bloodied cub.

He also sees her with his night vision goggles and raises his rifle at her: a Franchi Momentum Elite. "What the hell are you doing out here, girl?"

"I..." Mary doesn't know what to say.

He actions his bolt to chamber a new round and eject the spent cartridge he just used to murder the cub. "Now, very slowly, drop that bow and your arrows."

Mary nods. She doesn't look down at me but keeps her eyes on him as she flings the bow away, and then the quiver—

So that they're within my reach. But when the quiver hit the ground, the arrows tumbled out—

All are beyond my reach except for one.

And one is all I need.

Camo Guy clicks his tongue as if he's genuinely regretful. "You sure are a beauty. But, hey, you saw something you weren't supposed to, so…."

I'm crawling slowly, inch by inch, toward the closest arrow.

"I…I won't tell," Mary vows.

I've got the arrow and am sliding it toward me. But because it's in my left hand, I'll have to shift the arrow to the right hand and the bow to the left.

Camo Guy chuckles at Mary's offer. "Well, now, considering I can do hard time for snagging this little fellow, I just can't take that chance."

"Can I at least say a prayer?" Mary's voice is trembling, yet she's doing the right thing: stalling.

Camo Guy sighs. "Jeez! … Oh, alright, already. But make it quick."

His eyes are on Mary, so he doesn't see me rising to one knee and sighting him.

"Thank you, sir." Mary clasps her hands. As she raises them to her chest, I draw—

Then release—

Only to see my arrow whiz by him.

Shite!

"What the…" Angrily, Camo Guy swings the gun in my direction, sights me—

And then he gasps.

I look up just in time to see him drop to his knees—

Because Mary's knife is lodged in his chest. He looks down and sees this too, before falling face down.

Mary drops to the ground beside me. All the blood has left her face. She's quivering so severely that I can barely comfort her in my arms. In time, she whispers, "I…killed a man!"

I raise her chin so that we're eye-to-eye. "To save my life."

Sobbing, she buries her face in her hands.

"He was going to kill you too," I remind her.

Mary nods. Her hands are still shaking as she drops them to her side. "Yes—it was self-defense," she sighs as she leans into me. "Still…"

"The first time you take a life isn't easy, I know."

"Really? Do you remember your first kill?" She pulls away from me. "Tell me the truth: was it *ever* hard for you? How many kills have you made since then? Fifty? A hundred?… *A thousand?*"

I shrug. "Definitely not a *thousand.*"

Mary stares at me, abhorred. "When did you quit counting?"

I think for a moment. "When I realized 'how many' no longer mattered. What's important is why. Mary, it's not always 'me versus them.' It's them versus us. By 'us,' I mean the citizens of our country. I'm saving lives by killing those who wish to cause mass murder. I've accepted that assignment." I take her hand. "But that doesn't mean you have to."

"I know, Mom." She turns to stare at Camo's dead body. "What should we do about him?'

I rise and walk over to him, then turn him over, but only to pull Mary's knife from his body. As I wipe it clean on his jacket, I say, "Let's just let Mother Nature take its course."

We're not fifty feet away before we hear them: Mama Bear and the cub who got away.

Their howls for the fallen cub echo through the trees scaring the birds, who take wing to a less mournful place.

Even knowing the deer is just a few feet away, I imagine they'll take out their grief—and hunger—on Camo.

To ensure I'm right, I take note of our coordinates to give to Abu Nagashahi, my wet work operative at Acme.

What happens in the forest stays in the forest.

PREVENTING ATTACKS: THE BEAR FACTS

FOR PREVENTION:

• NEVER keep food and toiletries inside your tent! Bears smell anything that has a fragrance. Instead, purchase a "bear bag" to store these items. Everything should be individually wrapped in plastic bags, specifically Lok-Sak or Op-Sak, which are leak-proof, odorless, and air-tight.

• Hang the bear bag on a tree (out of reach for bears), at least 100 feet from your tent.

• Also: prepare and eat your food at least 100 feet from where you'll sleep.

• Don't sleep in the clothes that you wear while cooking and eating your food.

• And don't forget: bring bear spray and a loud whistle.

IF YOU'RE ATTACKED:

• Don't Run. Experts say walk away slowly and sideways.

• Don't Panic. Talk calmly to the bear (don't shout), so it's not threatened.

*• If Attacked: With **brown bears** (like the grizzly, hump-backed, and found in mountainous regions), lie down in a cannonball position, and play dead. Fight back if it's **a black bear** (it has no hump and is common to all regions). Strike at the bear's face with anything you can find.*

Of the Manners Born

No matter the occasion or the situation, impeccable manners are a must!

In these increasingly trying times, it's tempting to forgo such niceties. But I beg you, kind ladies and gents, even as the rest of civilization crumbles around us, strive to do your best to adhere to these three tenets that separate us from lesser species:

Tenet 1: Greet others with a smile. Entranced by your kindness, they'll never see the knife coming.

Tenet 2: Keep a civil tongue. Cursing like a banshee is the biggest giveaway that you're about to attack. Declare your distaste only when you're close enough to stick the shiv in their gut. (Perhaps in a sly whisper so that those around will never believe it was your hit—unless the weapons have your fingerprints on them. All the more reason to wear fashionable gloves.)

Tenet 3: Always be a good hostess. As such, no one will ever suspect that the sugar lumps in your tea service are laced with Ricin.

I'M LYING ON A LOUNGE CHAIR IN THE BACKYARD, TRYING very hard not to listen to the argument between Mary and her boyfriend, Evan Martin, since they're in his room over our garage.

Okay, yeah, maybe I'm here because I want to know if Evan succeeded in finding out why Mary flip-flopped on her decision to take a summer internship with the University of California-Berkeley. There, they would have been working side-by-side. Instead, she's accepted the internship proffered by our friend at the NSA, Mario Martinez, where she'll be working at the Capitol.

Considering Mary's reaction to her first human kill, I was gobsmacked by her decision. "Mario insists it's strictly an office job," she told me. "And, frankly, I'm relieved about that."

"But the Berkeley internship will keep you just as safe, if not more so," I countered.

"Let me put it this way: I need to get away from…well, from here—Hilldale. I want to see what else life has to offer."

She means she wants to get away from me.

From *this life*.

I nod as if I understand. But no: I'm genuinely hurt.

Evan slams the door on his way out. As he clamors down the stairs, I exclaim, "Wait! Aren't you going to join us in taking Mary to the airport?"

"No, sorry, Donna. I'm heading back to Berkeley. Your

daughter has made her decision, which doesn't include me."

"It's just for the summer months. But when she comes back—"

Throwing open his car door, he snorts, "What makes you so sure she will? You know, she's just as upset at you as she is at me—and in either case, I still can't understand why!"

As his car screeches out of the driveway, "I mutter, "Welcome to the club."

Evan loves Mary, and I know she loves him too. Having a row right before going away for two months isn't what either wanted.

Did she even kiss him goodbye?

Will I get the same icy treatment before she heads to the plane?

A moment later, Mary starts down the steps. At first, she doesn't see me because she's too busy wiping away her tears. When she does, she averts her eyes.

"Honey…I'm sorry that—"

"Mom, please! This has nothing to do with you." She swats away the thought like it's a pesky fly.

Okay, more like a pesky parent. "You say that, but after our trip—"

"Please! Just believe me, okay? I'm doing what's right for me." Sighing loudly, Mary adds, "You know, you really don't have to take me to the airport. Dad can do it alone."

"Of course I do! The whole family wants to see you off!"

"Yeah, okay… whatever."

Before I can say another word, she heads into the house.

"That's got to be Mary's plane." Jeff points up at a Boeing 757 with the Delta logo on its tail.

We're standing on Dockweiler Beach just below Los Angeles International Airport. "See how it flew west over the ocean before banking back toward the east, then north?" he adds. "Los Angeles is just a latitude below DC, but thunderstorms are hitting the Midwest, so it may have to go further north—"

Trisha snorts. "Jeez! Who made you the official weatherman?" She stares to his side. "Next you'll be putting up your hands as if you've got a weather map, and pointing it out!"

"Trisha, dear, Jeff is only trying to help us visualize Mary's route," I point out.

Trisha pouts. "Big whoop. He's such a know-it-all!"

Jeff tweaks her nose. "Then I guess that makes you an ignoramus."

She slaps his hand away. "Quit mansplaining—*and* manhandling me! *So* unwoke—and so is calling me stupid!" She points both hands at her brother and then taps her middle and index fingers on each as if cutting him with imaginary scissors. "There—*you're officially canceled!*"

Jeff holds out both fists and pounds them together. "Oh yeah? Well, so are you!"

Jack steps in between them. "Alright, already! Enough

with the brother-sister act." He looks down at Trisha. "If I heard correctly, you started this fracas by jibing Jeff about playing weatherman."

Jeff snorts. "Ironic, isn't it? Considering that she's dumb enough to stand out in a rainstorm. And for that matter, she wouldn't know longitude from latitude if her life depended on it."

Jack gets in Jeff's face. "As for you, making fun of her only adds fuel to the fire. You turn sixteen in a month, which makes you two years away from being a legal adult. Why not act like one?"

Jeff nods resignedly. "Sorry, Dad."

"That's better. What say you drive us home?" My husband tosses Jeff the car fob.

I grimace. Jeff is a good driver, but once we hits the 405, things may get hairy with the highway's typical stop-and-go traffic and the broiling weather Looney Tunes driver drama. Still, I force a smile and nod. "Great. Trisha, Aunt Phyllis, and I can share the backseat."

"Not me," Aunt Phyllis announces. "I'm sitting shotgun on this wagon train." With a smirk, she wags a finger at Jack. "But no backseat canoodling! We don't want Trisha picking up any bad habits—at least, not from you two amateurs."

Trisha's reply sits somewhere on the Richter Scale between a yelp and an outright groan. She stalks off.

Her real frustration—that her bestie, Janie Chiffray, will be out of town for at least another week—has her crankier than I've ever seen her. Janie's dad, Lee, our former President of the United States, has taken Janie and her little brother, Harrison, to his cattle ranch in the Midwest, where he grew up. Before they left, he also told me that he, too, needs to reconnect with his roots. "I started a foundation in that region that supports a soup kitchen, a homeless shelter, and a farmer's cooperative. While we're there, we'll be visiting these organizations so that they can see how we all can make a difference. I hope they'll come back appreciating even more what they have."

I commend him for that.

Maybe I should have taken him up on the offer for Trisha to join them. It would have been an eye-opening experience for her too. Instead, knowing that she was already jealous of my one-on-one trip with Mary, I thought it would be better for the whole family to spend the rest of the summer together.

Hopefully, my plan won't be short-circuited with some crisis needing the finesse of my employer, Acme Industries. I'd much rather spend the next few weeks attending their team games (baseball for Jeff; soccer for Trisha), grilling in the backyard, and flopping down on a lounge chair beside Hilldale's community pool with a great book in my hand.

We've been inching forward on the 405 for about a half hour as Aunt Phyllis plays deejay. In other words, changing channels continually, even in the middle of songs. Suddenly, she turns around and announces, "By the way, Donna: I texted you a reminder of your matron-of-honor duties and heard nothing back." She flips down her car visor to give me an evil-eye stare.

She's marrying one of the officers in the Chiffrays' Secret Service detail: Porter Crosby. In fact, he's one of the agents assigned to Janie and Harrison.

Yikes!

"Um... When did you send it?" I ask.

"Before we left for the airport!" Aunt Phyllis frowns. "And a month prior to that. And on a Sunday every week in between."

"Oh…kay. I've had my phone on silent. You know, trying to be 'in the moment.'"

As if.

"You've had your phone on silent mode for over a month?" Aunt Phyllis's skeptical scowl would scare Godzilla. "Or have you just muted the texts from me?"

"Never!" I cross my heart.

Liar.

To prove she's now got my complete attention, I look down at my cell. Her missives are there, alright—along with three messages, all from work, and all with the exact code words:

TIME TO MAKE THE DOUGHNUTS!!!!!

Jack's cell has also been pinging. He sighs. "Let me guess. It's Arnie's day to send the bat signal."

I guffaw. "What was the giveaway?"

"His favorite food." Jack rolls his eyes.

Arnie Locklear, one of our mission team operatives, has

a silly sense of humor. If he weren't such a savant (perhaps I should preface that with *idiot*) about all things technological, one of us would have slapped him senseless long ago. As it is, he's saved both our arses on numerous occasions, so he's spared a free ride on the Donna and Jack terror train.

Smiling sweetly at Aunt Phyllis, I vow, "Give me a few days to look over your list and get back to you with some ideas."

"What do you mean, 'a few days?'" Her head twists around so quickly that I wince. I've seen that signature move only once before: from Linda Blair in *The Exorcist.*

"The very first line item is the date: in two weeks —*HELLO, McFLY!*" Aunt Phyllis screeches.

I harrumph, "Well, since I haven't even opened it yet, I wouldn't know that, now, would I?"

"Already, you're mucking it up!" she counters.

Jeff has let the car to our right go in front of us. The car behind us beeps the horn.

Aunt Phyllis sticks her arm out the window. I can't see it, but I assume she flipped the driver a bird because he's now laying on the horn.

"Sorry," Jeff mutters.

"It's not your fault," I reply. To prove it, I kick Aunt Phyllis's seat. "I promise I'll look at it when I get back from work."

"*Work?*" Aunt Phyllis's shriek is a clarion call to the drivers around us, who blast us with a cacophony of horns. "But *times a-wasting!* I've waited almost seventy years for my wedding day, and I ain't getting any younger—"

Someone yells, "*Shut up already, old bag!*"

Yet again, my aunt's arm goes out the window—

But Jack wrestles it back in before she can maneuver another one-finger salute—

And he doesn't let go. "Listen here, Bridezilla," Jack growls, "Donna will be home before dinner. At that time, the two of you can have a real conversation without starting a riot"—he nods in Jeff's direction — "or getting us in a wreck. Capiche?"

Aunt Phyllis bites his arm.

"OW!" Jack yells.

More horns blare.

Another driver shouts, "What the hell is going on in there?"

Jack reaches for the door handle—

Just as Jeff pulls forward and into another lane, which, miraculously, is suddenly wide open.

Trisha taps Aunt Phyllis on the shoulder. "'Almost seventy?' But… you told me you're only ten years older than Mom."

"Ha! That's because your mom is older than she lets on."

Aunt Phyllis's bald-faced lie earns her my middle finger—

Which Jack grabs between both hands before the kids see it.

Not that anyone is looking. Jeff's terrified gaze is

straight out the windshield. As for Trisha, she scowls out her window.

No one says another word until we pull into our driveway in Hilldale, at which point Trisha, Jeff, and Aunt Phyllis slam their doors as they vault from the car.

"That went well," Jack murmurs.

I shush him with a kiss. When we finally resurface, he adds, "You know, Aunt Phyllis's stress is compounded by the fact that Porter is out of town with the Chiffrays."

"Yikes! I hadn't thought of that." I sigh. "In hindsight, maybe I should have agreed to let Trisha join them. And I'm sure Lee wouldn't have minded if my aunt had tagged along too. Porter is the consummate Phyllis-Whisperer. He would have talked her out of her bridezilla shenanigans. And with all the golfing Lee has planned, she'd have made a great addition to his foursome. He's in awe that her handicap is better than his."

"Too late now," Jack points out. "No matter. She'll get over it. And besides, as Arnie puts it, 'time to make the doughnuts.'"

He's right. Next stop: Acme.

$$3$$

The Perfect Guest List

You can't be a hostess if you have no guests. Ergo, take out your favorite lined pad, a pencil, and your address book so that you can start the process of whittling down the list of those minions you know are salivating to be in your entourage at this very special soiree!

How do you decide who makes the cut? Here are two fundamental rules:

*1: **It depends on the event.** For example, a themed costume party — say, "Vicars and Tarts" rules out those who really are people of the cloth or the harlots in your neighborhood. Reserve the former for a more subdued event (except if it falls on a day of worship) and the latter for everything else. (No need to get ugly rumors started that your besties are sluts.)*

*2: **It depends on your maximum capacity.** If it's an open house, no problem: keep the food coming, keep the drinks flowing, and keep the drunks out of the pool. Set a start time and pray they leave before tomorrow's sunrise.*

The same goes for a pajama party.

However, if you only want a party of eight—and it's not a matchmaking scheme—pick fascinating conversationalists. If it is a set-up, do the same and pray the lucky lady or gent who has relied on you to choose their next mate has the good sense not to solely be led by their libido.

"I can handle more guests—as long as they're the right ones" you say? Then I suggest you put the rest of the names into a hat and draw.

That's what you get for being so popular.

"You're late," our boss, Ryan Clancy, growls at us.

"Traffic," I reply.

Dominic Fleming looks up from his seat, where he's texting. "Odd. It only took me twenty minutes. Considering I live around the block from the Craigs, and I arrived in plenty of time to make a cuppa—"

As Jack passes him, his elbow smacks into Dominic's head. Dominic's hand shakes, which makes him spill his cuppa.

"Criminy, old boy! No need to get your knickers in a twist just because I'm being honest about it."

"Honest, eh?" I ask. I point at the screen on Dominic's cell, which is in clear view. "Ah! Then I suppose your current heartthrob, Jody Keleske, is aware of the liaison you've just arranged with your friend with benefits, Teddy Twala. 'Got ya covered'? I guess we all know what that means." I wag a finger at him. "Tsk, tsk!"

Startled, Dominic puts the device on the conference room table.

"To set the record straight, Ms. Twala reached out to Dominic on behalf of her employer, MI6," Ryan huffs. "This morning, while you two were gallivanting around, there's been a bit of a crisis. Our cousins have intel that the U.S. missile program has been compromised."

This certainly gets everyone's attention. Abu looks up from his new obsession: the daily Wordle quiz. Ryan's pronouncement has even hushed Arnie and his wife—Acme's ComInt director, Emma Honeycutt—who have been bickering about whether their four-year-old, Nicky, should be signed up for T-Ball like Arnie wants. (Emma's argument: "Sports makes kids competitive bullies, not to mention the parents take it *waaaay* too seriously!")

Ryan taps a button on his console. A man's face appears on the conference room's wall-sized screen. He's tall, broad-chested, and hawk-nosed. His light hair is slicked back. The man has piercing blue eyes. "This is Stepan Bychkov. He's a Russian diplomat who arrives stateside in two days, ostensibly to justify Putin's invasion of Ukraine yet again in a speech at the United Nations."

"Hey, did you know that his last name literally means 'bull' in Russian?" Arnie pipes up. "We're teaching Nicky the language with adorable little animal flash cards—"

"We're trying to stay on point, Arnie!" Ryan roars.

Emma drops her head with a sigh.

"According to MI6, his real mission is to rendezvous with an operative embedded in the U.S. who will be handing off a thumb drive listing the coordinates of our country's four hundred active missile silos," Ryan continues.

"Well, that's not good." By stating the obvious, Arnie earns a withering glance from Ryan.

"And let's not forget that Russia will be aiming at the most obvious targets too: not just the White House, the Pentagon, and Camp David but McClellan Air Force Base in California," Ryan continues.

"Can we attack back in time?" Dominic wonders.

"Our silos are equipped with Minuteman III missiles, which have a max range of 8,700 miles and a max speed of MAC 23—that's around 17,500 miles, or enough to get it to Moscow," Ryan explains. "So, yes, as long as its inertial navigational guidance system hasn't been tampered with."

"The codes are changed often, aren't they?" Emma asks. "As well as the military personnel who have their fingers on the button?"

"Yes, on both counts. However, the concern is that Russia's hackers can compromise the algorithm used to create the codes. Just as dangerous is the revelation of the names of the military service personnel who work at the missile silos. They and their families can be harmed or blackmailed," Ryan replies.

"Should Bychkov succeed in his mission and the United States is disarmed, we'll be a sitting duck for Putin's objective," Jack points out.

"If Russia is doing its damnedest to infiltrate our defense system, shouldn't we assume it's doing the same with the other NATO countries?" I ask.

Ryan's scowl deepens. "Putin made it clear that all of

Europe is also on his hit list, NATO be damned. Believe me, MI6 has expressed the same concern and is doing its own reconnaissance in the U.K. Other NATO countries are following suit."

Jack lets loose with a low whistle. "So, stopping Putin before his operative liaisons with the traitor giving him the intel is tantamount to keeping him from world domination."

"Something like that." Ryan concedes. "In fact, two suspects have been identified. One is giving Bychkov the intel on the missile silos. The other will receive a thumb drive containing a virus that feeds Russia our launch code changes. But because of concerns that their immediate arrests will foil the U.S.'s counterintelligence mission—putting misinformation in Russia's hands—Acme will make the exchanges."

I ask, "Wouldn't that be an FBI op working in tandem with the CIA?"

"Under normal circumstances, yes," Ryan replies. "However, at the highest level, there appears to be a leak on our side. Until it's plugged, Director of National Intelligence Marcus Branham has tasked this assignment to Acme instead. We're to secure the thumb drives containing U.S. classified intel and hand off ones with fake intel in their place. We've got to come up to speed quickly too. Bychkov arrives tomorrow morning from Moscow. He's scheduled to address the U.N."

When Ryan touches the remote again, a woman's face appears on the left side of the screen, and a man shows up on the right. "The two possible suspects ID'd by MI6's intel will also be in New York the day after tomorrow." Ryan's laser falls on the woman: gaunt-faced, my height, and perhaps a few years older than me. Her frizzy blond hair is barely contained by her topknot. The blouse under her boxy suit is buttoned all the way up. Her cat-eye glasses make her pursed smirk look even meaner.

"For the past fifteen years, Myrna Fulham has been an administrative assistant at USSTRATCOM—one of the U.S. Military's unified combatant commands," Ryan explains. "It is headquartered out of Offutt Air Force Base in Nebraska, responsible for global strikes and strategic deterrence." Ryan's laser now points at the man. "Richard Seymour is coming up on his thirtieth year in civil service. He's a mid-level Pentagon tech department wonk."

I take a good look at him: perhaps mid-fifties, although his thick helmet of hair has nary a gray strand. He's fit, wears an expensive suit, and sports a pinkie ring with a large diamond.

"Mr. Seymour has expensive taste," Dominic points out. "The suit is from this season: a Brioni."

"Considering that his stay-at-home wife's taste is just as expensive and they've got three kids in private prep schools, my guess is that he's living way above his pay grade," Ryan adds. "Like Bychkov, both suspects have booked different hotels just a few blocks from the U.N. Neither has yet to purchase a tour ticket, but that can be arranged the day of their visit. Neither is aware of the other from the chatter between them and Bychkov on a secure chat app. They've been scheduled for separate meetings. You're to intercept them before their rendezvous with Bychkov, secure the intel, and replace it with trojans that allow our surveillance and havoc." He nods toward Arnie and then Abu. "Mutt and Jeff here will be next door, ready to upload the intel to Acme ComInt and Mario Martinez at the NSA. You'll then substitute the fake intel— for one thumb drive, an alleged coding algorithm; for the other, a list of fake eye-in-the-sky soldiers. Both have viruses that will wreak havoc with Russia's secure cloud."

Arnie hoots raucously. "And Acme will have punked the Russians twice this year!"

"A hack by an anonymous 'rogue' allows DNI Branham and President Libby Kentfield to claim clean hands," Jack reasons.

"Why isn't Bychkov staying at the Russian consulate?" I ask.

"I found that strange too," Ryan concedes. "Then again, neither of our suspects would want to be captured on CCTV anywhere near the consulate. Either Bychkov will rendezvous with them somewhere privately—or there will be an agreed-upon drop location. He nods at Abu. "By passing as hotel maintenance staff, you and Arnie will plant eyes and ears in the targets' hotel suites. After they check in, we'll send in the honeytraps." Ryan's eyes shift to me. "Though Richard is married, he doesn't let that stand in his way of playing the field. Our reconnaissance on his credit cards shows that he prefers the hotel bar for pick-ups instead of local watering holes."

Dominic smirks. "But of course. Why go out when there's a comfortable bed a few floors above?"

"Takes one to know one," I mutter.

Dominic's face turns red. His mouth opens and stays there. He's hard-pressed for a rejoinder.

"Donna, when you're alone with him in his room, hit him with the Love Potion and ask him what we need to know to either clear or indict him," Ryan says.

"Got it," I assure him.

Since the demise of the DNI's Intelligence Science Board, Acme has taken over some of its mandates: that is to say, our company develops and studies controversial technologies that won't necessarily pass a human rights sniff test. Acme's Love Potion is a perfect example. By the time this truth serum in a perfume-sized spritzer wears off, I'll be long gone and merely a pleasant fantasy.

"Dominic, you'll be Myrna's honeytrap," Ryan says.

Dominic frowns. "I say, old man, perhaps Jack would be better suited for the task."

Jack snorts. "When have you turned down a chance to charm some gal off her feet?"

Dominic lifts his head proudly. "Since I became a one-man woman."

The rest of us are laughing so hard that even Ryan's bellow, "Control yourselves, people! ..." at the top of his lungs doesn't shut us up—

Until we see Dominic's glare and realize it wasn't a joke. Finally, he glances at Ryan. "I hope you take me seriously, sir."

"Ah, sweet love!" Ryan sighs. "It's a many-splendored thing—*except in espionage.* So do what the Craigs have learned to do: suck it up. Either take on this mission as ordered, or find something else you're good at—perhaps working as a concierge at some five-star *Traveler*-rated hotel."

Harsh.

Dominic's jaw drops.

But soon enough, it closes again. He nods. Mission accepted.

One can't be an International Man of Mystery if one's job consists merely of wrangling hard-to-get show tickets and restaurant reservations for wealthy tourists.

"If Ms. Keleske is the right woman for you, she'll understand what you do for God and country." At least this time, Ryan's tone is less condescending.

Our boss now turns to Jack. "Abu, Arnie, and you will bug Myrna and Richard's suites. You'll be in the room adjacent to Richard's, while Abu and Arnie will take the room adjoining Myrna's. That way, you'll be right there for Donna and Dominic if anything goes wrong."

While they're still under sedation, we'll substitute the fake intel for the real deal. Dominic and Donna will put GPS microdots on them so that we can track them to the drop location."

Jack gives him a thumb's up. "What's the game plan if either Richard or Myrna admits to being the traitor?"

"Afterward, the FBI swoops in and arrests the suspects for espionage. But of course, Bychkov won't be detained during their drop-offs. We want the fake intel to make it into Russian Foreign Intelligence's secure cloud." Ryan pulls two thumb drives from his pocket. He tosses one at Dominic and the other at me.

Seeing how Dominic is smarting from Ryan's reprimand, I figure it's best to show a stiff upper lip. I force a smile. "Easy-peasy."

"Famous last words." Ryan retorts.

Yeah, okay, I get that he's not buying it.

He looks at his watch. "Get moving, people. You've got a flight to catch to the Big Apple."

WE'VE JUST PULLED INTO HILLDALE AND ONTO OUR STREET when I remember: "Aw heck! I've yet to look at Aunt Phyllis's bridezilla list!"

"Well, it's too late to turn back now. Look."

Jack is right: Phyllis sits on one of the veranda's Adirondack chairs. She's arranging a vase of pink roses: perhaps a gift from her fiancé, Porter.

I groan. "Breaking the news to her that we're leaving town is sure to wipe that smile off her face."

Jack sighs. "My suggestion: send her a text after we're over the Rockies."

"Coward," I grumble. "No, I just have to be straight with her. After we review her must-do list, I'll give her a reasonable timeline for each task."

"I'll do some of the legwork too," Jack suggests.

"Really? You'd do that?"

"Sure. Just because I don't have two X chromosomes doesn't mean I can't tap my softer side."

"If you can help me keep her sane between now and the wedding, I'll tap it for you—although I doubt it'll stay soft for too long." I prove it with a kiss on his lips.

"You're on," he declares.

We've just gotten out of the car when Jody comes out of our front door holding a tray laden with five tall glasses of lemonade. A social media consultant, she played an integral part in the success of our last mission when our team went undercover as social media influencers. Sparks flew between her and Dominic, setting off a five-alarm love affair.

Trisha follows with a platter of chocolate chip cookies. She's laughing at some aside told by Jody's wards—twelve-year-old twins, Genghis and Guang—are relaying in unison. It's so funny that they all crack up even as they interrupt each other.

Seeing us, Phyllis waves us over with a big smile.

Jack and I stare at each other. "Let's enjoy Aunt Phyllis's good mood while we can," Jack suggests. "That is until you give her the bad news that we're pulling out later tonight. Maybe, like, just before we run out the door to hop in the car."

No need to ask me twice.

I've barely made it up the porch steps before Aunt Phyllis says, "Aren't these beautiful? Dominic sends Jody two dozen roses every week. She wanted to share some of them with me!" She points at Jack. "When was the last time my niece got flowers from you, young man?"

Jack's mouth drops open. "It's been too long. But I do have other surprises for her—"

Phyllis reaches up to cover Trisha's ears. "Not in front of the kiddies, sir!"

Trisha rolls her eyes. But when she moves away from

my aunt, it's only to kiss her on the cheek. She then exclaims, "Hey, Mom, guess what? Jody has offered to help Aunt Phyllis plan her wedding! You know, she's coordinated, like, a bazillion celebrity events—and at least five I-Do's for social media influencers! And the twins and I are helping out. We're going to learn calligraphy to address the invitations, and we'll get to taste-test the food and the wedding cake—"

"Oh… well… I see." I pause just a moment: *Thank you, Lord.*

Then I meet Jody's gaze: She gives me a sly wink.

Hmmm…

Dominic is right to want to hold onto this one. In fact, I'll murder him myself if he ever messes up this relationship.

"Sorry, Donna," Aunt Phyllis shrugs, but there's no remorse in her tone. "I know you were looking forward to having this bonding experience with me. But hey, life's too short to cater to sentimentality when the biggest event of my life is just a few weeks away."

"Oh!... Um… Well, yeah, of course, I'm disappointed. I mean…" My voice trails off because I'm now laughing so hard that tears are rolling down my face.

I guess that beats shouting "Hallelujah" at the top of my lungs or breaking out in a happy dance.

"Aw, baby, did I make you cry?" Phyllis holds a napkin to my nose. "Blow hard…*HARDER.* Can't have you sniveling all over Jody's home-baked cookies just because you're broken up over it. Not to worry! She may be helping me plan the wedding, but no one will replace you as my matron of honor." Aunt Phyllis throws her arms around me. "Or as the daughter I never had."

Now I really am crying.

"Since Mom died, that's always how I felt about you too," I whisper between sobs.

I know she hears me because now she's crying too.

"Just stay safe," Her whisper is fierce, her eyes darken with concern.

She knows why Jody offered.

My sacrifices are made for my family too.

Another reason to love my aunt even more.

"And get home in time to try on the maid-of-honor dress Jody picks out for you—because I know if she leaves it up to me, it may be so risqué that you'll get arrested before you make it inside the church." Aunt Phyllis dabs a napkin to my wet cheek.

"Cross my heart," I vow.

4

Hospitality

Hospitality and manners go together like 1000-*count Egyptian cotton sheets and goose-down pillows: ideally, they work in tandem to create a delightfully relaxing experience!*

Besides hearing a pleasant "Hello!" from the check-in desk, some free goodies—warm cookies, a bottle of wine, a free massage—are an excellent way to welcome visitors.

A towel warming rack in the suite's bathroom is always a plus, as is a turn-down service and chocolates on your guest's pillows.

Such niceties don't have to be an occasional getaway experience. Follow your favorite hotel's example of hospitality when welcoming guests to your home.

However, should your visitors get too comfortable, politeness can be abandoned to make the point that they've overstayed their welcome. Gentle reminders can include itching powder in their bed and otherworldly moans in the middle of the night.

If they still don't get the hint, the next time they empty your best bath salts to soak in your oversized tub, throw a dryer into it with the gentle warning that next time you won't forget to plug it in.

MYRNA'S HOTEL IS JUST A BLOCK AWAY FROM RICHARD'S AND positioned kitty-corner from the United Nations Headquarters, which takes up five blocks on Manhattan's First Avenue, between 41st and 45th Streets.

And yet, our targets are worlds apart.

Richard's temporary abode is a brand spanking new five-star cloud-scraping world-class hotel. I'm sitting in its large, sumptuous bar, right off the hotel's lobby and at the entrance to its banquet-cozy Nuevo Cuisine-touting restaurant. Today I'm a redhead in a curve-hugging silk emerald-green sheath with spaghetti straps that gives its neckline an ample peek-a-boo plunge. To take full advantage of the dress's side slit, I've placed a stiletto-heeled foot on the empty bar stool next to me.

This hasn't deterred a few men from asking, "Is this seat taken?"

Each time, I coyly nod and answer, "Sorry, yes."

Jack, equipped like the rest of us with earbuds and contacts that transmit all we see and hear, chuckles from where he's waiting: on the other side of the locked adjoining door to Richard's suite.

In contrast, according to Dominic's miffed mutterings, Myrna's hotel is a hovel. "Seriously, it could be a rabbit's warren! One is forced to share a *communal bathroom*! I'll eat my proverbial hat if she's truly a mole."

"Oh, please make it the red suede Stefano Ricci top hat," I implore him. "It's not like you wear it, anyway."

"Don't be ridiculous! That would be *the last* of my chapeaus I'd consider doing away with. In the right setting, it's a veritable showstopper."

"You're right about that," Jack mutters under his breath. "Like, say, a Halloween contest. Not that we'll ever know since you refused to lend it to Arnie to top off his Willy Wonka costume."

"Don't be imbecilic!" Dominic huffs. "Had you any taste at all, you'd understand why *Savile Row Magazine* raved about it—"

"Yo, Romeo, show time," Abu's voice breaks through. "Myrna is entering the lobby now—to your left. The security cameras have been looped, so no better time for a meet-cute."

"On it," Dominic mutters.

He's dressed like an academic: jeans, a button down shirt under a fitted but casual jacket, and wire-rimmed glasses. After the front desk clerk hands Myrna her room key, Dominic goes to the elevator and taps its button. She's still struggling to push her oversized suitcase while juggling her large purse and a computer bag when the elevator opens.

"Hold it, please!" Myrna shouts.

Dominic turns, as if seeing her for the first time, but acquiesces with a tentative smile, "Yes, of course."

As the elevator doors close, he asks, "Which floor, madam?'

"Oh…" Myrna sees he's already pushed the button to the seventh floor. "Same as yours, I guess."

No one else will ring for the elevator. Abu has assured this by putting a "BROKEN" sign on all the other floors.

As the elevator rises and Myrna futzes with her bags, Dominic spritzes her with an unscented version of Acme's love potion. By the time they reach the seventh floor, Dominic's suggestibility test—his offer to wheel her suitcase into her room so that she can manage her smaller bags —is met with a meek "Yes, thank you."

Dominic is right. The suite is barely big enough for a bed and a desk, let alone Myrna's humongous suitcase.

As he attempts to hoist the suitcase onto the desk, he asks, "What's in there, a dead body?"

"No. Just six dresses, four pairs of sneakers, eight pairs of panties, nine bras, a few books, my hiking boots—"

"Now that we know the potion is activated, ask her something pertinent," Ryan barks.

"Will you be meeting with Stepan Bychkov?" Dominic asks.

Before Myrna can answer, Emma says: "Donna, you're in play! I'll mute all other operatives but Jack and me."

"Duly noted," I whisper.

I catch Richard out of the corner of my eye surveying the patrons from the bar's raised lobby. I'm in luck. I'm the only woman who isn't part of a ladies-who-lunch-late threesome, of which there are several in the banquettes scattered throughout the lounge. Feeling his gaze, I lift the toothpick spearing two olives from my almost-empty martini glass, examine it for just a few seconds, then slide it into my mouth. One of the olives is now between my lips.

I turn to Richard. Our eyes meet.

He gets the message when my tongue rolls the olive into my mouth.

By the time I've swallowed it, he's reached my side. "Is this seat taken?"

"It is now."

I'm about to move my leg so that he can take it, but he puts his hand on my thigh. "Stay put."

"Do I have to?" My plea comes with a come-hither smile.

He laughs. "Why? Do you have somewhere else to be?"

I slip my hand under his jacket and tweak his nipple under his shirt. "That's up to you."

Hint taken. Richard takes my hand and leads me to the elevator.

EVEN BEFORE THE ELEVATOR DOOR HAS CLOSED, HE'S SLAMMED me against its back wall. As he grinds his mouth into mine, his hand roams up the slit of my dress. Thank goodness Arnie has rigged this rising box to be an express train straight up to Richard's floor: the seventy-fifth. I'd hate to have an audience right now.

When I hear Jack's curse, I remember my wish hasn't been granted.

"All in a day's work," Emma reminds him.

With that in mind, I shove Richard off long enough to mutter, "Sorry, but a little Binaca might make your kisses a bit sweeter." He scowls at the slight but only nods when I pull out the love potion and murmur sweetly, "Open wide."

The spray goes up his nose, causing him to gag. "What the…"

"Oops! My bad," I coo. "Let me make it up to you." To make good on my promise, I manhandle him below the belt—

Yikes! He's supersized and rock hard….

When we reach his floor—the penthouse—he's deflated and docile.

Perfect.

The door opens, clearing the air of the love potion. I can breathe easily: figuratively and literally.

Dazed and confused, Richard doesn't fight me as I steer him down the hall toward his suite: one of two at the very end. I suppose Jack is in its mirror twin.

At my directive, Richard taps the lock's eye with his key. The door opens.

Nice pad indeed…

The sliding doors to the terrace, which runs the suite's entire length, are open, allowing a brisk breeze, which is par for the course seventy-five stories high.

"When are you to meet with Stepan Bychkov?" I ask.

"Soon," he murmurs. "Ninety minutes." Sweat drops from Richard's brow.

"Where?" I ask.

"We are to meet…at…" Richard is now breathing heavily. "Um… Why are you asking me this?"

"Aw, heck!" Emma mutters in my ear. "Close the terrace doors! The fresh air is clearing his head of the love potion's effects!"

As I move forward, he backs up. In no time, he's on the terrace. Between deep gulps, he shouts, "Who are you?"

I pull out the spray as I run toward him. He backs up against the railing, then runs the length of the terrace, stumbling between the wrought iron furniture. I follow, but between my heels, my tight dress, and dodging through the terrace's furniture maze, I can't reach him before he ducks into the master bedroom, locking the sliding door between us.

Shite!

I run back to the living room door in the hope of getting there before he locks it too—

Or runs out of the suite.

Instead, I find Richard sprawled out on the floor. He now sports one hell of a shiner.

Jack is rubbing his knuckles.

Gently, I take Jack's hand. "Want me to kiss it and make it better?"

"We can't let Richard rendezvous with Bychkov." Jack grimaces as he raises his hand out of the bowl of ice water where it's been soaking.

"What…? Are you suggesting that you meet Bychkov

as Richard?" I look up from the task at hand: tearing Richard's suitcase apart as I hunt for the thumb drive that he's to hand off to Bychkov. Jack has already frisked him. It's not in the clothes hanging in the closet, either.

Still knocked out, our captive has his wrists and ankles shackled with Zip Ties and a gag in his mouth.

"I can whip up a face mask in a jiffy." Arnie weighs in. He sits cross-legged on the floor with Richard's computer in his lap, scrolling through its texts, emails and chat apps.

"Richard and I are the same build," Jack reasons. "Besides, it's all we have time for."

I shrug, but what can I say? He's right.

Arnie adds, "And now that I've decoded the Signal correspondence between them, we know where the meeting is to take place: the dive bar across from this hotel —a place called Smiddy's." He stares down at the computer screen. "His secure cloud is almost wiped clean of the stolen intel. Still, I wish we had found the SD card he's to hand off to Bychkov. Ryan won't like that it's out in the wild."

"I found it!" Triumphantly, I hold up an open condom wrapper and pull out its contents: not just a condom but an SD card too. I hand it to Arnie, who puts down Richard's laptop and grabs his own. As his fingers click away on the keyboard, Jack studies the condom box. Sneering, he exclaims, "'Extra-large?' Who does he think he's fooling?"

"I'm just happy I never got to find out," I mutter.

Arnie giggles as he uploads the thumb drive's contents

to Acme's secure cloud so that the Pentagon can verify that it is the missing intel.

A moment later, Emma comes on the TV. "Ryan is putting out a pretty big fire. Instead, I'll connect you to DNI Branham, who has been sent your reconnaissance and will validate that it is indeed the stolen data."

My eyes shift to Jack and Arnie. From the look on their faces, they're just as perplexed as me.

Branham's face fills the screen. "You've got it. Thanks for the save, Acme. Now spread the kitty litter." His face dissolves into Emma's.

Instead, Bychkov will receive Acme's thumb drive containing the misinformation.

"We've now got everything except Ryan's confirmation that the FBI will be alerted when to tail Richard," Jack looks at his watch. "Where the heck is he, anyway? Already we're cutting it close. Only forty minutes until the rendezvous."

"You want my blessing to double as Richard? You've got it." Ryan's voice comes from the suite's built-in television monitor, as does his image. He sighs. "Here's hoping Bychkov won't suspect anything is wrong."

Arnie sprints into the adjoining suite to grab the mask-making kit.

"I assume, then, Myrna has been cleared?" Jack asks.

"Nope. Worse than that, she's dead."

"What?" Jack exclaims.

I add: "But…how? Did Dominic have to—"

"I wish he had," Ryan declares. "Myrna passed out. When she came to, he was carrying her toward the bed.

She freaked out, grabbed the gun from his back holster, and shot him first. With him bleeding out and the rendezvous with Bychkov, she must have realized she was in over her head"—he hesitates—"so she turned the gun on herself. Bullet to the head."

A wave of dread rolls through me. "Dominic...*is dead?*"

"Not yet. But he's in a coma. Abu got him to the hospital just in time."

Thank God...

Oh dear—I've got to let Jody know...

"Arnie, we'll need you to make two masks: one for Jack —and one for Donna," Ryan says.

"You mean to say Myrna was supposed to meet with Stepan Bychkov too?" Jack asks.

"Yes. After Abu secured the real intel and got Dominic to the emergency room, he returned to Myrna's room for wet work. He scanned her face from all sides. Emma has just relayed the shots to Arnie. Donna, Abu is on his way over with your wardrobe and the fake intel. Your rendezvous with Bychkov will take place just a block from Smiddy's. It's an apartment in a three-story red brick walkup over a deli. The building and apartment keys were in her possession. Obviously, they've met there before, so we can assume Bychkov carries a similar set."

"How do you know this?" I ask.

"Myrna had a burner phone in her possession. Just before she died, she received an encrypted message from Bychkov, in Russian: '*Ozovyye trusiki, moya lyubov.*'" Ryan pauses. "It translates as 'pink panties, my love.'"

"Let me guess: Myrna has a pair like that in her suitcase."

"Frankly, they're pretty flimsy, and I don't think they're your size. I mean that in a *good* way…" Ryan's voice dies off. "An SD card was wrapped inside them. DNI has confirmed its intel is the list of our country's missile silos."

"Which means Richard was to hand off the launch code algorithm," I reason.

"Affirmative. Each silo should correspond with one of the algorithms on the card Richard was supposed to hand off to Bychkov. Myra's SD card has an additional encryption as well. ComInt is attempting to break the code now." Ryan sighs. "Donna, it's up to you and Jack to save the US missile system."

"Just another fun day in the neighborhood," Abu mutters.

5

Meet and Greet

FIRST IMPRESSIONS MEAN EVERYTHING!

That being said, there are a few graces you can bestow on those you meet for the first time. For example:

***1: Don't come empty-handed.** Gifts are always appreciated and are an indication of your innate thoughtfulness. (They are also an excellent way of re-gifting. Think of it as an impromptu game of "White Elephant," except that you already know your recipient.)*

***2: Always open with a nicety.** "My, that's a pretty dress" or "What a beautiful name you have" is always appreciated. No need to tell them what you really think unless you catch them flirting with your hubby. At that point, a few choice words will have them thinking twice about what they give up when they've gotten the reputation of neighborhood slut.*

***3: And finally, mind your manners throughout the visit.** The phrases "Please" and "Thank you" give you great mileage in Pleasantville. Sure, the time may come when the newcomer* *becomes more frenemy than friend. Until then, hold your powder and don't shoot until you see the whites of their eyes.*

"Wow, you could have fooled me into thinking you were the real deal!" My shudder at Jack-slash-Richard is involuntary.

I'm looking at his mirror image because Arnie is positioning the prosthetic nose that will make me Myrna's doppelgänger. At least, it's Jack's voice. But since he's already got on his game face—that is, Richard's Seymour's smug mug—I have to squelch the urge to wince even as I stare at him.

"Not to worry. He's still passed out on the bedroom floor," Jack replies. He tosses me Myrna's infamous pink panties: a tiny lace cotton-lined triangle held in place by a thin pink elastic.

"Once he has the fake intel in hand, I'll make up some excuse to scare him away," I promise. "To be perfectly honest, I didn't like Bychkov's directive to you either—I mean to Richard. You're supposed to sit on the bar stool the farthest from the front door, ask for a particular brand of beer out of a can, drink it, put the SD card under the empty can, and then wait for the bartender to hand you a pouch of loose diamonds?"

Jack shrugs. "I assume the beer's name is obscure, which makes it a workable password."

I shake my head. "Something just doesn't ring right."

"It's set up as a dead drop, so our guess is that Richard

has never laid eyes on Bychkov, and our target wants to keep it that way," Jack counters.

"I could understand that. If Richard has nothing else to offer him, why risk a face-to-face? The liability is too great."

"I hear ya," Jack admits. "And doll, remember: Abu will be shadowing me. He's not a boy scout in many ways, but in emergencies, he always comes prepared."

"True that," I concede. "So, Arnie and I are supposed to babysit Richard?"

"Just until I get back. Now, how about a kiss for good luck?"

I make sure that it's a long, lingering affair. When we part, Abu is leaning against the wall, grinning. He carries a rucksack. "Show's over, lover boy. Let's boogie." As he waves to me, he adds: "Don't head out to Bychkov's love nest until we get back. We'll be shadowing you too."

I watch with Arnie on his computer as he monitors Smiddy's webcams: the real action instead of the loop that I assume he'll put in place to cover Jack and Abu's tracks from when they enter to when they leave. One webcam shows the alley in back of the joint. Three others, from interior webcams high on its ceiling corners, capture the bar's interior. The last one captures any traffic to or from the restrooms.

While Jack enters through the front door, Abu goes in through the back a few moments later. The place is only partially filled, so he has no problem finding an empty booth and sliding into it. Smiddy's few patrons are riveted by the big-screen monitor over the bar, where a

Warriors-Lakers playoff game is in its final neck-to-neck quarter.

In the meantime, Jack has already ordered the bag of chips and the beer in a can. He asks for a glass with it.

When I sit down on the couch, I kick something—

Richard's briefcase. It's open because Arnie or Abu had already gone through it. I feel something odd under the exterior lid—

A hidden flap. When I open it, I find something tucked inside:

A photo: Richard—naked with Bychkov. They have some woman in a manwich:

Myrna.

Yikes!

I snap my fingers at Arnie. "Quick! Inform Jack and Abu that Richard does indeed know Bychkov—and Myrna too—intimately, in fact, on both counts."

"On it!" Arnie exclaims.

He's relaying my message just as the bartender gives Jack the beer and the glass. As Jack pops the can's lid, Abu meanders to the bar and orders a beer on tap and a whisky chaser. He stands next to where Jack is sitting, but they ignore each other. Just two strangers in the night.

A moment later, the bartender sets Abu's drinks on the bar. Jack motions the bartender to take his tip and slides the empty can to him.

The bartender's sleight of hand is so smooth that I can't see him pocket the SD card. He walks back to the register with Jack's cash. In the meantime, Abu swaps out the beer glasses, taking Jack's back to the banquette along with his whiskey chaser.

When the bartender returns to Jack, he has his change and the bag of chips.

Jack opens the bag, shakes it, and smiles. I guess the diamonds are in there.

In the five minutes Jack has taken to down his glass of beer, Abu has already taken off. The glasses he leaves on the table are empty.

A few minutes later, Jack also heads back to Richard's hotel.

JACK ARRIVES FIRST. WHEN HE MOVES IN TO KISS ME, I PUT UP my hands, crossing my index fingers as if hexing him. "Face off first."

"Oh yeah, I forgot." He pulls off his mask.

Ten minutes later, Abu enters. Immediately he opens his rucksack. It holds a canister and a small packet, which he slices open, pours into one of the canisters, caps it, and then shakes. When he takes off the cap, he glances inside. "Donna called just in time. Her instincts were right. Bychkov's endgame was to poison Richard. It would have induced a heart attack within a half hour of drinking it."

"So, now the Feds will wheel him out in a gurney, bagged and tagged, and Bychkov will think he accomplished his goal: killing an asset he no longer needs," Jack suggests. "In the meantime, Richard serves twenty-to-life for treason."

I clap my hands. Jumping up and down, I exclaim, "And we get to keep the diamonds!"

Arnie lights up. "Really?"

Abu snickers. "As if."

"What's your guess: are they real?" I ask.

"I wouldn't bet on it," Jack replies.

"Me neither," Arnie retorts.

"Ditto," Abu says. "But there's one sure-fire way to find out." From his rucksack, he pulls out a jeweler's loop. Taking the pouch of diamonds over to the desk, he adjusts its lamp and then inspects one of the diamonds. "Nah. A good fake, but not the real deal."

I laugh. "Do you always carry a jeweler's loupe with you?"

"Sure. You never know what you'll find at a lawn sale or a flea market. Let me tell you: when it comes to gems, I've found some real beauties," Abu insists. "My retirement goal is to open a jewelry store"—he stares at me with puppy dog eyes—"unless Donna finally takes my offer to partner on a pie shop franchise."

I snort, "You'd better hold onto that loupe 'cause the pie shop ain't gonna happen." I turn to Jack. "What about Richard?"

My husband nods toward the bedroom. "By now, Ryan has already alerted Branham of the op's success. I'm sure the FBI is on its way over to pick up Sleeping Beauty. The Bureau will also have eyes on the bartender at Smiddy's since he was complicit in the handoff. They'll arrest or turn him into an asset if he's an embedded Russian cell. Acting as a double agent is better than jail time."

"Until Bychkov learns he's been turned," I reason. "If there really is a mole implanted on the highest level of our government, he won't last long—"

I'm interrupted by the ping of Myrna's burner cell. Looking down, I add: "She's been summoned by the Puppet Master."

"Then we're off to the races," Jack says. "Not to worry, Donna. We're in your eyes and your ears. Should anything happen, we're just a few seconds away."

My mind goes to Dominic, who's now lying in a coma.

Famous last words.

I ENTER OUR RENDEZVOUS LOCATION THROUGH A DOOR ON THE far side of the deli.

The stairwell is narrow. Its carpet is worn and dirty.

Classy, right?

I only knock once. The peephole goes dark while the viewer assesses me.

When the door opens, Bychkov pulls me close to him— so quickly that it takes my breath away. He's taller than he looks on the monitor, and his shoulders are broader. I wish I could use the Love Potion on him. By the way he's flexing his hands—as if he's itching to put them around my throat—I could use a diversion.

Over his shoulder, I glance around the room: it's a studio at most: café table and chairs for two but no monitor or couch. One amenity is its Juliette balcony, which is open now since it's stifling, and this joint has no air conditioning, but it does have a small galley kitchen on one side and a bed on the other—

California king. Large enough for a menage-a-trois.

Like the one Bychkov had with at least two of his turned assets.

Hungrily, Bychkov nuzzles my neck. "I watched as you strolled over. I couldn't wait to get you into my arms."

The long plane ride from Los Angeles gave me plenty of time to practice Myrna's husky Nebraska delivery. "First things first," I reply. I pull away. Then, from my low-cut pink bra, I pull out the SD card and hold it out to him between the index and middle fingers on my right hand. When he reaches for it, I take a step back. "I'm glad you hadn't planned on tag-teaming me tonight. I want you all to myself."

"I'm sorry the oaf was so rough with you."

"No, you're not!" I retort. "You enjoyed every moment of it."

He shrugs. "You're right. You turn me on when you squeal with pleasure. But I love it more when I'm the one making you ecstatic."

"Good. Then you can make it up to me now." I pull his tie so that we're lip-to-lip.

His kiss is chaste—more like a kiss-off. Something tells me he's not as enthralled with Myrna as she'd hoped.

He steps back, flinging his arm toward the small table by the settee, where two glass flutes flank an ice bucket holding a bottle of Krug Brut Rosé Champagne. "First, we celebrate. Pink champagne, your favorite! And, of course, the chocolates you love."

"You've thought of everything," I coo.

Bychkov nudges me over to the table, where he picks up the bottle and pops its cork. After pouring the fizzy fluid into the flutes, he offers me one. "Here's to you, my darling."

No way in hell will I drink this.

I smile. Does he see my lips trembling?

I'll trip and spill it on him. Or create a diversion and exchange our glasses—

Nope, can't do that! We don't want him dead—

I take the glass.

Bychkov's smile widens. Picking up the other glass, he says, "Cheers, sweet Myrna."

In tandem, we raise the flutes to our lips—

The bang on the door is loud and doesn't stop. "Gas leak! Open up! Immediately!"

I recognize Abu's voice.

Bychkov scowls but heads over.

Because his back is turned, he doesn't see me sprinkle the contents of my glass all over the grimy carpet.

Suddenly, in my ear, I hear Arnie say, "Go to the window—quick! And jump!"

Um…

What the hell?

Four stories…

Really?

Jack's voice booms in my ear: "Donna, hon, just do it —*now!*"

So I do.

AH! TAKING A LEAP OF FAITH:

I've jumped out of a plane with a parachute on my back, knowing that I had a few seconds in which to pull the cord that would release a nylon canopy and allow me to float a bit more gently than the freefall that started the journey.

I've fallen down an elevator shaft, blinded by its darkness and my fear, forcing myself to reach out and grasp for anything that would save my life—and for doing so, I survived.

To escape my ex-husband-slash-terrorist Carl, I dropped into the Gulf of Mexico from the top of a hotel.

Then there was the time Carl bound my ankles and wrists and tossed me into Puget Sound—

But I digress. What I have to do now is to trust that when I fall, it won't be directly onto the back alley's asphalt road—

And, thanks to Jack and Arnie's quick thinking, I don't. Instead, I land on a heavy-duty inflatable airbag.

Jack helps me onto my feet and then shoves me toward a plain white panel van at the front of the alley. "Get in the back with the monitors. Lock it behind you," he commands.

I listen in on Abu arguing with Bychkov to evacuate. Through the monitor, I watch as Arnie upends the airbag, leaning it against the building under Bychkov's balcony so that it's out of sight—

While Jack unrolls a rug. Myrna's body flops out.

When Bychkov looks out his balcony, he'll find her there: eyes open and glazed, arms and legs akimbo.

The hole in her skull is up against the asphalt. It lays against a thick liquid substance meant to look like blood.

Arnie and Jack jump into the van. Jack barks through Abu's fire department walkie-talkie: "Attention all units: the leak is contained. The tenants have been given the all-clear. Repeat—*tenants are in the clear.*"

Through the monitor pointed at Bychkov's balcony, we watch as he appears and looks down. Seeing Myrna, he scowls.

In less than five minutes, he's out the building's front door.

Abu chortles, "I guess the FSB will have to find a new safehouse."

A minute later, he, Jack, and Arnie have deflated the airbag, and Myrna's body is now rolled in the carpet.

Five minutes later, I've called my dear friend, Jody, to tell her that the man she expects to walk through her door any moment with a bouquet of pink roses is lying in a hospital bed fighting for his life.

Jody hangs up the phone, sobbing.

6

Event Planning

Every great hostess is a consummate event planner!

That being said, these three tips will help you join that very elite club:

1: Serve plenty of food, glorious food! *Give the beasts the wildest feast! Stuff them to the gills so that they wobble when walking away! Does this mean you'll be sweating over a hot stove for several days prior? Not necessarily. Just put out your best silverware, china, and crystal, order the best take-out in town, dish it onto your finest serving platters, and voila—the next day, you'll be the talk of the town!*

(Especially if one of your take-out orders gives your guests ptomaine poisoning. Helpful hint: Check your city's restaurant health code violations list before serving. Just sayin'.)

2: **Come up with a festive theme!** *Let the weather be your guide. Or choose a theme that fits the time of year. Better yet, be creative! Ask your guests to dress up as a character in, say, their* *favorite novel, be prepared to perform creatively, or perhaps be ready for a fast-paced game night.*

In other words. Keep it fun, irreverent, and silly!

(Unless what you're planning is a funeral. If so, do the opposite of all posted here. A theme party based on dressing up as the dearly departed may be original, but it will also be cruel—as would turning their wake into a game night. Shouts of "Bingo" during the eulogy will be abhorred.)

3: Pay attention to all details. *Even the smallest ones cannot go unattended. Yes, the menu is essential. And sure, the ambiance must perfectly set the mood. But if your guests find even one thing off-putting, word of it will run through the room like wildfire.*

That's not to say you can stop such snark in its tracks. Of course, you can! Suggestion: lock the room. Start the fire.

Problem solved!

"I'M GLAD JODY HEARD ABOUT DOMINIC FROM YOU," RYAN tells me.

"Don't sell yourself short. I'm sure you would have delivered it just as sensitively." I try to smile, but the message dies on my lips. "Ironically, Trisha had texted me that just before I called Jody. Lee offered up Lion's Lair for the ceremony and reception, and Phyllis had narrowed down the honeymoon location to three resorts, all of which fit her exacting criteria. Jody insists on spending as much time at Dominic's side as possible, but at the same time, she sees Phyllis's wedding as a great diversion. Thank goodness she can do a lot online."

"Yeah, about that: I know you were looking forward to taking charge of your aunt's wedding"—his smirk is his tell that he's joking—"but you'll be otherwise engaged."

My jaw drops. "But—I thought the mission was a success!"

"And Part Two will be just as much fun."

"Hardee-har-har."

Ryan pats my shoulder. "Perk up. At least you're not in a coma—or planning your aunt's wedding."

"The former could still happen," I remind him. "Just knowing this, the latter now doesn't sound so bad either."

Ryan laughs as if I've said something funny. He's always had an odd sense of humor.

He nods toward the conference room. "Let's join the others."

Cheers and (from Arnie) war whoops go up as Ryan thanks our team for our successful pivot after Myrna's death.

Ryan holds up a hand to silence us. "Normally, DNI Branham would let Army Counterintelligence take it from here—that is, assess and eliminate the threat from within; and sniffing out the embedded Russian assets within or around the missile facilities. However, our friends at MI6 picked up chatter that indicates Bychkov was somehow forewarned that the substituted thumb drives attained from Richard and Myrna were fakes."

Our smiles fade.

"Worse yet, somehow, Bychkov could still attain the real intel. Realizing that his cover is blown, he's left the country. He's already passed it forward to his superiors."

"So, back-ups of the intel must have also been held elsewhere. And Bychkov was aware of this?" Abu asks.

"Apparently so," Ryan replies.

"But...how would he have known it was fake?" I wonder.

"It would have had to be analyzed by someone who would know the difference," Ryan explains.

"That someone would have also known of our operation and informed Bychkov that he'd been burned," Emma counters.

"In other words, MI6 was right about our government's infiltration by a mole," Jack reasons.

"Looks like it. If only they knew who it was." Ryan frowns. "Branham already has a team searching for possible suspects. He's pointed in the direction of those high up the ladder to have access to this classified material. In the meantime, considering Putin's saber-rattling, time is of the essence." He sighs. "Acme will have to stop the stateside sabotage of the silos."

"But there's like, four hundred Minuteman III silos alone!" Arnie exclaims. "Not to mention over two hundred and sixty Nike missile bases."

"MI6 also passed forward another coded message that Bychkov was to deliver to Putin. Emma and the ComInt team broke the cipher just an hour ago. It lists the seven targets recommended by the mole, who goes by the alias 'Azrael."

Abu lets loose with a low whistle. "In Sikhism—and Judaism, for that matter—it's the name given to the 'angel of death.'"

"This asshole has a very high opinion of himself," Jack mutters.

"It's up to Acme to assure this asshole—and the world —that it's no more than an inflated ego," Ryan retorts. "On that front, we'll have some help." He buzzes his assistant, Natasha. "Please send in our guest."

When the door opens, I'm staring at Evan.

HE SHRUGS AT MY DOUBLETAKE.

I point to the chair to my right, which puts him between Jack and me. He blushes when I kiss his cheek. Too bad. He's family, so I have the right to act like a proud almost-mama. "I take it we're to be colleagues on this caper?"

"Looks that way. Apparently, you're a man down. And, as it turns out, since my company, BlackTech, has supplied the technical analysis to the Department of Defense's Missile Defense program, I'm the best person to detect any trojans in the missile launch software. But knowing that timing is of the essence, having Arnie as part of my blue team comes in handy."

Maybe it's a good thing that Mary went to DC after all.

What Evan is doing could put him in danger. Had she chosen Berkeley, she would have spent her time worrying about him. The fewer distractions, the better.

Hearing Ryan's growl for everyone's attention, Evan sits ramrod straight. Not that I blame him. Ryan can be scary. Still, no need to let Evan in on the truth: Ryan is as sweet as a teddy bear.

Unless provoked.

The brown bear and her cubs come to mind.

Seeing my shudder, Jack shows his concern by squeezing my hand, then whispers, "He'll be alright."

"Despite Evan's software maintenance, MI6's coded message left little doubt that assets have infiltrated the target locations to manually facilitate the breach's success," Ryan continues. "That's where the rest of you come in, thanks to Evan."

All eyes turn to him.

Evan clears his throat. "BlackTech was tasked with embedding access control software that monitors for and detects malicious activity. The bad guys don't know this because only DNI Branham is aware since he approved the installation and has yet to white-paper it to the White House. The timing couldn't be better. A few days later, a brute force attack was carried out on all the 400-plus missile silos. Several were breached with an insider's help."

"How do you know this?" Abu asks.

"The security cameras were disabled, and diversions were created to allow the assets to access the appropriate mainframe," Evan replies. "A base can have as few as ten and as many as fifty silos. Though they are left unattended, video monitoring and other intrusion detection mechanisms are in place."

"What is the damage assessment?" I ask.

"The attacks didn't breach the launch code firewall. However, it accessed other data, including the personnel, security, and shift files of those who work on the base," Evan replies.

"So, it's time to try, try, again," I reason. "They'll either attempt to compromise someone with their finger on the button or incapacitate them."

"Exactly. We'll need to cast a very wide net," Ryan counters.

"Do you think the embedded assets will try to compromise the base commanders?" Abu suggests.

"Depends on the new threat's delivery method. Compromised personnel could be anyone, even someone as innocuous as a janitor," Evan warns us.

"Which is a perfect opening to the great intel Acme's ComInt team." Ryan nods to Emma.

She shows her appreciation with a blush. "My team has been monitoring the social media apps used by the targeted base's personnel. We looked for phrases that may pass for coded messages. We've identified several possible targets—one in each facility on our list—all of which are in contact with one particular account. Its user identifies themself as 'WorldSaver.'"

"What are they saying to each other?" I ask.

"In each instance, WorldSaver commiserated with the targets' concerns over 'the end of the world.' None spelled out their proximity to our country's nuclear arms program until WorldSaver nudged it out of them, usually within a month into their online heart-to-hearts."

He nods at Ryan. Who taps the monitor's remote control.

A map of our country appears on the wall-size monitor. Immediately, several states enlarge on the screen: Montana, North Dakota, Nebraska, Wyoming, and Colorado.

"These are where our country's active missile silos are clustered. Just yesterday, the last of the Minuteman IIIs have been replaced by our latest, most efficient nuclear weapon, the Sentinel."

"So the sabotage has been perfectly timed," Jack points out.

"For Russia, yes. But now that we're tracking him, it also works in our favor. WorldSaver has scheduled six drops in six days. If we're lucky, we'll be on his or her tail the whole time."

"So, we're not to stop him in his tracks, only swap out our SD cards for his?" Abu asks.

"Affirmative. Though I wish it were the former, it works better for our counterintelligence efforts." Ryan shrugs. "While you three intercept the handoffs"—he points to Abu, Jack, and me— "Evan and Arnie will be uploading the trojan that will feed Russia misinformation." The monitor's map zeros in on Montana. "WorldSaver's first target is one of the thirteen silos in and around Winifred Montana, on various homesteads."

"Do we know which of the silos are in jeopardy?" Jack asks.

"No. But we know where the brush-pass is happening, and we'll be staking it out." Ryan chuckles. "The Central Montana County Fair, in Lewistown. The livestock booth during the 4-H Livestock contest. One of the BMATs—Rory Edgerton, a ballistic missile analyst technician—has a son with a hog in contention. He's got a pretty big family: six kids."

"He's our target, then?" Jack asks.

"Yes." Ryan's shoulders sag at the thought. "After the Russian asset's brush pass with his handler, one of the Craigs will create a diversion, allowing the other, or Abu, to steal the SD card and replace it with the one containing the fail-safes coded by BlackTech. Even before Russia's turned asset installs it, Evan and Arnie will assess the intel its virus was to deliver so that they can emulate its coding. That way, it will feed Russia the misinformation provided by DNI Branham. BlackTech's security gives them cover as tech consultants. If necessary, Branham can give Abu, Donna, and Jack the clearance to go undercover as missileers—that is, base personnel."

"And then onto the asset's next assignation," I reason.

"Yes. From there, WorldSaver heads off to Jim Creek Naval Radio Station in Oso, Washington," Emma explains. "The facility, under the auspices of the Naval Computer and Telecommunications Area Master Station's Pacific Command, sits on almost five thousand acres of forests and rolling hills. It's our country's strategic communications center, which sends out very low frequency coded radio transmissions to our nuclear submarine fleet."

"After that, WorldSaver heads back east to our worst-case scenarios: Malmstrom Air Force Base near Great Falls, Montana; Warren Air Force Base near Cheyenne, Wyoming; and Minot Air Force Base, near Minot, North Dakota," Ryan adds.

"All are 'Missile Alert Facilities,' or MAFs." Evan explains. "Besides storing nuclear warheads and cruise missiles, fighter squadrons are posted at these bases."

This order is met with silence and tight-lipped frowns.

"With all due respect, sir, it'll be like looking for a needle in a haystack," I declare.

Ryan nods. "This brings us to the biggest stack of all: Offutt Air Force Base near Omaha. The host station to the 55th Wing: the largest of the USAF's Air Combat Commands. Besides other very significant affiliated units, it houses USSTRATCOM, a.k.a., the US Strategic Command Headquarters."

"In other words, Putin wants to run the bases," Jack mutters.

"And only Acme stands in the way of him hitting the ultimate home run." Ryan stands. "You'll be wings up at 0100 hours, so get packing."

For Jack and me, first things first: stopping at the hospital to check Dominic's progress.

And to hold Jody's hand.

We've just pulled into the hospital parking lot when Jack's cell buzzes. "Mary?...Yeah, hi, hon. Are you settling into DC okay?"

She called Jack, not me.

Yes, I'm saddened but not surprised.

Jack reads my shrug correctly: follow Mary's lead, even if I don't get to talk to her.

To that end, he murmurs words like, "Good…Great…"

Until the giveaway: his eyes shift my way and then move back as he mutters, "No issues, all good." (Pause, then louder): Ah, excellent! Sounds like it's right up your alley…Yeah, okay, kiddo, no issues. Get back to work. Thanks for checking in. Love you."

We sit silently. If he thinks I'm going to beg to know how she's doing, he's wrong…

Instead, I ask outright: "Don't be stingy. Throw me a bone."

Jack sighs. "She's settling in. Mario hooked her up with a couple of other interns looking for a roomie, so all good there. She's working as an aide in Senator Chad Bennington's office."

"From Nebraska, right?"

"Yep. Upstanding guy. Former Air Force pilot, in fact."

"Nebraska. Ergo, Omaha. Ergo, Offutt AFB." I tap onto Senator Bennington's website. "Well, whaddaya know? He just so happens to be the Ranking Member on the Arms Services Committee."

Jack sighs. "What's your point?"

"Mario got her the assignment. Ergo, he's using her as his mole."

Jack groans. "Quit saying 'ergo.'"

"But I'm right, aren't I?"

He kisses me—long enough to shut me up.

I like when he finds a solution we both enjoy.

When our lips part, he mutters, "You didn't hear it from me."

"Yeah, yeah, I know. As far as Mary's concerned, I'm in the doghouse."

"Not exactly."

"What are you not telling me?"

"Whatever it is, I'm going to keep 'not telling' you if it means kissing you all night—or at least, until we're wheels up in, like, a couple of hours."

"I'd rather we continue this conversation in bed," I admit. "But since we can't, I guess the next best thing is to pray Mary stays safe, despite whatever op Mario got her to agree to, which, kudos to him, is pretty persuasive, considering she doesn't like the dirty stuff. Speaking of dirty stuff, I'm glad you didn't mention Evan's role in our mission."

"You bet I didn't. It would have been wrong on so many levels. First off—again, I'll neither confirm nor deny this—but if, in fact, she's Mario's eyes and ears in her new position, the last thing I need to do is divulge Evan's mission, which is also top secret. Secondly, what they say to each other is solely between them."

"So, what you're saying is that she doesn't see me as 'the bad guy?'"

"*Hmmm.* Define 'bad guy.'"

"The one who's been teaching her things that will later make her hate herself—like how to kill."

"Great question." Jack puts his arm around my shoulders. "In truth, you're teaching her to protect and defend—not just herself and those she loves, but in defense of her country. It's not fun. It ain't pretty. And it sure as hell is scary—all things someone who has just turned eighteen shouldn't have to worry about. But this is the world we live in. Ignorance is not bliss. Someday she'll thank you."

"I hope you're right."

"Aren't I always?"

I kiss the grin off his face.

Yep, that shuts him up.

JODY IS HOLDING DOMINIC'S HAND—THE ONE THAT, UNLIKE the rest of his body, isn't hooked up to the various paraphernalia monitoring his fight to stay alive. Dark circles now surround her eyes, which scan the page of the book she reads aloud in a soft, sweetly clear voice. I recognize the passage from *The Prisoner of Zenda*:

If love were the only thing, I would follow you—in rags, if need be—to the world's end; for you hold my heart in the hollow of your hand! But is love the only thing?

A solitary tear rolls down her cheek. She only realizes we're standing in the doorway when she wipes it away. She puts the book down and then nods her okay to enter.

Jody doesn't anticipate our group hug of grief. She doesn't know whether to laugh or cry. "I...I've been trying to hold it together for Dominic. I was doing okay—until now." She steps away, now wiping both cheeks with both hands. "Before his...his injury Dominic was reading *Prisoner of Zenda* aloud to me. Claims it's his favorite book of all time. He felt two men were living inside him: the devil-may-care bon vivant assassin and the other a quiet, gentle man who just wanted to find his soul mate and live happily ever after." Jody drops her head. "I'd always wondered if Assassin Dominic would win out."

"The fight isn't over," I insist. "Dominic's medical condition has stabilized."

Jody stares at me. "They don't know if he'll ever come out of this coma. If he does, I want him to know I'm here. And... if he doesn't... I'm at his side until the end." She drops her head again.

Jack and I look at each other. We're thinking the same thing:

I'd do precisely the same.

When we turn back to Jody, we see that a weak smile has risen on her lips. "I knew you'd understand. As for Aunt Phyllis's wedding, she's locked, loaded, and ready to go. Trisha and the twins really came through. In fact, Aunt Phyllis is reciprocating."

"How so?" I ask.

"Lee Chiffray claims he doesn't want Porter mooning around for his bride-to-be, so she's invited to join them at the Chiffray family ranch." Jody hesitates: "I know she'll be calling you to break the news—and, with Lee's blessing, to see if you'll approve of Trisha and Jeff joining her there. Of course, she knows your mission takes priority."

"Well… if the kids don't mind—" Just then, our cells buzz in unison.

"It's Trisha," I say, as Jack exclaims: "Jeff's calling."

Before we have the chance to say a word to them, they're babbling to us:

Trisha can't wait to join Janie: "—and we'll be horseback riding and fishing—"

As for Jeff: "We can drive quads! And Mr. Chiffray says we can learn to rope calves!"

Then together, they beg: "So…can we go?"

Jack and I are so stunned that the kids yell: "Hey! Are you still there?"

"Yes, okay. Have fun," we answer.

They squeal in our ears before hanging up.

Jody puts her arms around us. "You have it all. Someday, Dominic and I will too."

WHEN WE'RE BACK IN THE CAR, JACK SAYS, "WHERE IS THE Chiffray family ranch, anyway?"

I chuckle. "You got me. He always struck me as a city slicker." I text Aunt Phyllis:

ME

Congrats on getting the details tucked away—and getting a free pre-honeymoon with Porter. Although I

know dragging Genghis, Guang, Trisha, and Jeff isn't the most romantic way to spend it.

PHYLLIS

Not to worry! Those kids will keep busy. And they're thick as thieves! Jeff and Genghis are smart as whips—and very competitive. Better than that idiot, Cheever, right? And from what I hear, Chiffray Ranch is a lux dude ranch, so they'll be safe.

ME

BTW, where is Chiffray Ranch located?

PHYLLIS

The closest town is Glenwood, Iowa. On the Missouri River but his land backs up to hills and forest. And near an ancient earth lodge! The boys are nerding out about it. Almost excited about this as the local raceway. Go figure.

ME

Have a blast!

After reading this to Jack, he declares, "Good. Far away from all the drama."

I feel the same way.

7

When Mayhem Ensues

AT ANY FUNCTION, THE HOSTESS SETS THE TONE. HOWEVER, *when mayhem ensues, she'll be further tasked to specifically withhold any indelicate behavior in public. By following these three very important rules, you should rise to the occasion with aplomb:*

*1: **Move others out as quickly as possible.** Breathe deeply, then take a good look around. While others are panicking, perhaps use a not-so-gentle voice that reinforces the severity of the situation and insists that they follow your directions to the letter.*

(That being said, you're excused this time for not having calligraphed or embossed the necessary tidbits on heavy paper stock and hand-delivered before their arrival. Makes sense when you think about; it. Had you done so, no one would have RSVP'd.)

*2: **Take charge.** Whereas decorum is always the hallmark of a proper lady, emergencies allow one to bend the rules a wee bit.*

For example, if there are naysayers present, one shot from a small revolver into the ceiling should make a believer of them. For those who still poo-poo your warning and insist on partying on, a closer call with a bullet may finally get their attention.

*3: **Leave no guest behind.** Like a good hostess, you'll need to make sure that all your guests have left your doorstep alive and well, even if they have to run for their lives to do so. Before leaving, as quickly as possible, do a sweep of the premises. (Word of caution: don't blame yourself if things get tits up—unless someone ends up that way.)*

*4: **Even if it's not your party, in an emergency, a gracious guest—you—always chips in.** During the incident, take a moment to assess your hostess's state of mind. Feel free to step into the role if you find her incoherent, comatose, or dead. (Unless you killed her. If so, go on the lam.) There is no better time to exert your reputation as THE go-to gal in any situation —especially one that is out of control.*

JACK IS DRESSED IN JEANS, A SHORT-SLEEVED PLAID SHIRT, shit-kicking boots, and a ten-gallon hat. I wear cat-eye glasses and a red wig braided into pigtails. We hold hands and lick homemade peppermint ice cream from hand-rolled waffle cones as we meander from one booth to another, oohing and ahhing over the livestock on display at the Central Montana County Fairgrounds in Lewistown, Montana.

We're really shadowing Rory and his wife, Ramona Edgerton—both in their late thirties—and their enormous brood. Big with child, Ramona strolls their youngest, two-year-old Rhonda, while tempering the rough-and-tumble antics of their twin boys, Ricky and Randy, with threats of withholding funnel cakes and other sugar-fueled sweets for the day. There is also eight-year-old Rhonda, ten-year-old Robby, thirteen-year-old Rhianna, and fifteen-year-old Ronnie. The entered hog, Big Boy, is Ronnie's 4-H project. He's also earning an extra letter grade in his science class.

While helping his eldest son spread extra hay through the hog's pen, Rory chats with the passersby who call out his name. None linger, nor has he walked over to anyone. He grimaces as his eyes scan the roving crowd. His finger taps nervously on the hog pen's top rail.

Yes, he's anxious.

He should be. From what we've read of his conversations with WorldSaver, somehow he'll be passed an SD card containing the trojan that will allow Russia to hack his silo's launch codes and change any directives given.

We've got to intercept it and hand off BlackTech's trojan instead.

There's a holster on practically every adult's hip because, unlike California, this state and those on our other stops while on this mission permit open carry. Our mission team's weapons aren't visible on purpose. We never want to pose a threat.

Abu has positioned himself on the other side of the pig's pen. He's dressed in a maintenance jumpsuit and a Billings Mustang baseball cap and carries a toolbox. "Anything yet?" he murmurs into mic'd earbuds.

All three of us have copies of the Blacktech SD cards.

We don't know the delivery system for the intel, so we carry the same intel on thumb drives and microdots.

Since we've got electronic eyes and ears on each other, all it takes is a slight shake of Jack's head for him to know the waiting game is far from over.

In the back of a van parked under a shady tree, Arnie and Evan monitor the fairground's security cameras. They've also got access to satellite surveillance in case (God forbid) something goes wrong, and we have to track either Rory or his Russian handler in the steady stream of vehicles flowing in and out of the fairgrounds' parking lots.

At first, I don't see the woman because she stands so close to two other women that one would think she's with them: slim, young, in shorts, with oversized sunglasses, and with short dark hair. But then she leans back just enough to place her arm against the pen's railing. Her gauzy white muslin top has wide, flowing sleeves.

Rory notices her too. But as she walks away, she leaves something behind: light brown, the color and size of a packet of raw sugar.

"It's her—shorts and white top, short dark hair," I mutter.

"We've got her sighted," Arnie assures me.

Abu bends on one knee as if tying a shoe. Instead, he opens his toolbox and tips it over—

Just then, Rory walks toward the rail—

Only to hear Rhianna and Rhonda scream, "Rats! Lots of them! Daddy, Big Boy's gonna eat'em!"

Ronnie grabs a rake and starts chasing them. There's

nothing Rory can do but follow his son's lead. Rats can give the hog a disease, so he has no other option.

Jack gives me cover as I swipe the sugar packet and swap out the memory cards.

By now, there's a crowd around the pen, laughing as they watch the excitement. We pretend to be a part of it. In reality, we're shielding the packet.

As the crowd thins, we move with it, leaving the packet still on the rail.

"He's got it," Abu tells us.

"And the asset?"

"In the ladies' room," Arnie chimes in. "And…*Yikes!* Ramona followed her in there! She's angry as hell!"

Jack and I look around. Rhianna is hovering over her little sister's stroller.

"Donna, you should see what's up," Jack insists.

I'm off in a flash.

THE LAVATORY'S DOOR HAS A WET FLOOR SIGN ON IT. I enter anyway.

From the anteroom, I hear shouting beyond the door to the stalls and sinks.

I inch open the door in time to catch Ramona growling: "—and you think you can get away with having an affair with my husband? Wrong, you bitch!"

She raises the gun in her hand. Her kill shot is only ten feet.

But when the other woman's eyes shift my way, so do Ramona's—

Which is the other woman's cue to lunge at the pregnant woman. She grapples for the gun, but Ramona holds tight—

Until the woman pushes her against the wall. The dropped pistol goes skittering on the tile floor—

Until I pick it up.

With it, I point to the other woman. "You—out of here!"

I don't have to ask her twice.

Crying, Ramona sinks to the floor.

I drop beside her. In time, her sobs become hiccups. At some point, she stares over at me. "I would have killed her, you know."

"And you would have regretted it. Your children need you."

She looks down at her huge baby bump, then back at me. The suspicion she had for the asset is now aimed my way. "How did you know I had more than the one?"

"I was in the livestock pavilion, admiring your son's hog. I thought you looked distressed. Because of your condition, I felt someone should ensure you were alright. I mean…you certainly have your hands full." I sigh. "Now I guess I know why."

Shamed, Ramona drops her head. "I've suspected my husband was having an affair for a few months now. He's gone a lot. That's part of his job. But… I thought he was in love with me, with the family we've created together." Her lips drop into a scowl. "I don't know who she is. I've never seen her around these parts; believe me, it's a very small place." Tears glisten in her eyes. "I guess she'll tell him I know about them."

"Good. Then he'll quit cattin' around because he realizes what a wonderful wife he's got—and doesn't want to lose her," I declare.

Her tears fall onto her generous breasts. "What if he loves her more than me? What if he wants to leave me for her?"

I sigh. "I suspect you scared her off for good. If so—and she tells him why—he'll know he needs to make amends to you." Gently, I lay my hand on her belly. "Let him do his best: for your family. For the time you have together. It's fleeting. We never know what fate has in store for us."

She nods, then lays her head on my shoulder.

I hope she takes my advice.

Be it a week, a month, or perhaps a year, Rory and Ramona will get a knock on their front door. Then Rory will be taken away by federal agents: to be tried as a traitor, convicted, and sentenced to jail time.

He'll miss seeing his children grow up and enjoying the simple pleasure of a family.

He may lose their love.

They will undoubtedly lose their respect for him.

I wonder why he did it.

Jack is waiting a few yards beyond the ladies' room door.

When he sees me, he holds out a bag. "A gift for saving our asses."

It smells delicious. I take a peek inside. *Hmmm.* "It doesn't look like anything I've ever seen before—let alone eaten!"

"Abu's now addicted to them: deep-fried Snickers. He's already on his way back to the airstrip. Hopefully, he won't have a stomachache on the flight. Since the plane only has one restroom, it won't be pretty."

"That good, eh? Then save some for Evan and me!" Arnie must be driving there, too, because the next thing I hear is him cursing at being stopped by an active cattle crossing.

"The target is driving away in a pick-up truck—and fast. I've got the license plate. It's a rental." Evan's voice is now in our ears. "We'll be tracking her via satellite to her final destination."

"I guess it'll be an airstrip that takes her to Oso, Washington, and the Jim Creek Naval Radio Station, same as us," I reply.

Cautiously, I take the bag. I pull one out and take a tentative bite. "Oh. My. Gawd! *It's heaven in a deep-fried crust.*" Still, I thrust the bag back at him. "You're torturing me! Aren't you afraid I'll lose my girlish figure?"

"If we're to accomplish what Acme has on our plate for the next week, trust me, you'll work it off."

He's convinced me. I've started on my second as we slip into our car. As I stuff my mouth, Jack revs the engine, and we're off.

I'M PHYSICALLY FORTY-ONE THOUSAND FEET IN THE AIR. BUT my mind is a million miles away.

Perhaps not that far: It's still back at the state fair.

Because our pilot, George Taylor, keeps the plane at a high enough altitude to smooth out any Rocky Mountain updrafts, the rest of our team is relaxing. Evan has curled up with a book on one couch and Arnie on another, playing a video game. Abu stretches out in a lounger watching the stock market gains on the Bloomberg channel.

The flight will be a short one. About two hours between Lewistown Municipal Airport and the closest private jet airport to Oso, Washington—Paine Field in Everett—is only long enough for a cat nap in Acme's Gulfstream G700. Jack, who has been nuzzling me in the plane's sole bedroom, sighs. He's no fool. He's noticed that my responses to his attempts at romance are lackadaisical, to say the least. He eases beside me and turns so that we're face to face. "What's on your mind, love of my life?"

"I'm thinking about the Edgertons," I admit. "What's your opinion: Was Ramona right? Did Rory do it for love? Or was it for the money?"

Jack shrugs. "Until this op is wrapped up—not by us but by the Feds—we won't know. If Rory was enthralled by the spy, shame on him. His wife is already wrangling six kids, with another on the way! His rapport with his children makes me believe he's a family man. My guess is that he got a financial offer he couldn't refuse. Think about it: those who fight our country's battles—be it on land, sea, air, or in Rory's case, as 'eyes in the sky'—are paid a pittance compared to a newbie analyst in the tech industry or on Wall Street. Considering their training and their important roles in keeping our military at its finest, their salaries should be competitive. No need to tempt fate because you can't feed your family."

"Agreed. Thanks for putting that into perspective." I snuggle into the crook of his arm. "I'm sorry he felt the need to sell out his country. I just hope it doesn't tear his family apart. The shame alone...." I choke up at the thought.

Jack holds me close. Together, we fall asleep—

But not for long.

Abu taps on our door and then peeks in. "Wake up, sleepy heads. Ryan has intel for us, like *now.*"

———————————————

8

———————————————

How to Encourage
Scintillating Conversations

———————————————

A GRAND HOSTESS IS ALSO A GOOD CONVERSATIONALIST! WHEN considering talking points, the rules of engagement are as follows:

1: Keep up with your guests' favorite topics of interest. *You should also be knowledgeable about current events, local news—and especially gossip! Word of caution: don't be a bombastic lecturer who never lets others get in a comment edgewise. At the same time, one mustn't come off as the Grand Inquisitor, either! As a scintillating conversationalist, be prepared to walk a fine line between moderator and interrogator. (The latter role is immensely more successful when cracking a whip. Talk about a conversation starter!)*

2: At all costs, keep the conversation going. *You can do this by knowing your guests' favorite talking points. For example, if one is a renowned Wiccan, by all means, ask her to demonstrate a charm or spell that works! If another has had a few brushes with the law, allow him to recite the plea bargain that* *freed him up to be at your soirée. Your other guests will indeed find it fascinating, if not outright hair-raising.*

3: Invite those who are both chatty and witty. *No hostess can be expected to carry on the conversation alone—not with everything else she must do to keep the party at its liveliest. Should you be forced to invite particular guests who are dull, be sure to include a couple of ringers who can keep the conversation flowing—*

Even if you have to pay them.

On second thought, if boring guests are on your list in the first place, it's time for new friends.

WE STUMBLE OUT OF BED AND TOWARD THE MAIN CABIN. Ryan and Emma are on the monitor. Our boss isn't smiling, but he waits until we're seated before barking tersely: "Sorry to disturb your cat nap, but I felt it was important to give you an update on your adversary. I'll let Emma give you the good news first." He nods to her.

Since he still hasn't cracked a smile, it can't be all that great. Jack must think this, too, because he grimaces as everyone leans forward, all ears.

Emma begins: "Thanks to Donna's face-off with the Russian spy in the state fair's women's lounge, Acme's facial recognition software could pick up enough morphological biometrics to put it through the DNI's intelligence database and pull up any known Russian operatives."

"How long will that take?" I ask.

"Hopefully, we'll have something for you by the time you land," Emma replies.

"Now for the not-so-great news," Ryan warns. "Acme SatCom shows that she drove to Lewistown's Medical Center. It has a multi-story parking deck, which is where we lost her. We assume she swapped cars there before taking off again, waiting until several cars left the structure simultaneously."

"Lewistown only has one airport," Jack points out. "I assume we continued monitoring the cars that headed there and all flights headed west toward Washington state?"

"Correct. Three private jets took off within the hour prior to your leaving and within three hours afterward," Ryan confirms. "Unfortunately, the airport parks its patrons' cars in hangars where their planes are kept."

"In other words, Acme couldn't ID the patrons either leaving their cars or boarding their flights," I grumble. "Did any of the planes end up at the airport nearest to Oso, Washington?"

"One headed for Phoenix," Ryan replies. "Another landed in Jackson, Wyoming. The third jet filed papers for Sacramento, but it's now headed further north. It looks like it's doing a direct flyover of the forty-two hundred acres that make up Jim Creek Naval Station."

"Our guess: her turned asset needs to be on their shift to give her access to what she needs," Emma explains.

"Or it may turn out that the sabotage is also a two-person job," Evan replies.

"The asset is careful that radar can't pick up the plane

at the altitude of fourteen thousand feet: the height needed for parachuting," Ryan adds. "The region is a 'no drone zone.'"

I'm confused. "I thought Jim Creek didn't have an airport or a landing field."

"It doesn't, which means the Russian asset will be parachuting into a viable drop zone inside the base," Ryan replies. "Not that there are many of those. The terrain is hilly and forested."

"Is there a way for Acme to track a parachute drop in the dark?" Jack asks.

"Our satellite can pick up a body's infrared flares, as can the security cameras mounted around the station," Ryan explains. "The facility is so small that it can be manned twenty-four-seven with only twenty-one officers."

I do the math. "So, essentially seven officers per eight-hour shift."

Emma adds, "We assume the compromised asset will have overridden the security cameras with looped footage. Even so, we've hacked into the system's live feed. As soon as we spot the Russian operative, we'll let you know if she's headed toward the station or rendezvousing near one of its numerous rows of transmission towers."

"And you'll be following her lead," Ryan informs us. "The Russian operative's accomplice will have turned off the aerial surveillance system so that her appearance goes undetected. We assume this contact has also secured credentials and a getaway vehicle for her. To that extent, you'll go in under the same cover. Otherwise, she may be in and out before you even land at the closest tarmac:

Paine Field, in Everett Washington, which is forty-five minutes from Jim Creek."

The words are barely out of his mouth when we feel the plane dropping lower and going slower.

"By the way, the facility also rents out its campgrounds to current and retired Navy personnel," Emma informs us. "We're sending you the coordinates to a couple of cabins secured under your aliases. Number 15, for the Craigs, is under the name of Jim and Janie Smith. Number 16, for the gentlemen, is for 'Tom Green, Jerry Blackthorn, and Roger White.' There you'll find backpacks with food and credentials and the key fobs to a couple of vans. It will prove you have a legitimate reason for being on the grounds, should anyone ask. You can drop the vans at Paine Field the next day, where George will be waiting for you."

"Get ready to jump, folks," Ryan proclaims. "And remember what they say: 'It's not flying. It's falling with style.'"

"Pithy,'" I mutter.

Landing in a dense forest in the dead of night—

I look out the window:

With no moon.

What could possibly go wrong?

ABU, EVAN, ARNIE, JACK, AND I ARE FLOATING IN A DARK SKY that is, thankfully, cloudless. And though we don't have a moon to guide us, galaxies of stars sparkle over the Cascade Mountain Range.

At least, I assume they do. I'm staring into the dark abyss beneath us. As we get closer to the tree line, our night vision goggles and GPS will help guide us away from the old-growth redwood trees that cluster the hills surrounding Jim Creek Naval Radio Station. We've avoided the biggest no-no: landing between the two rows of giant candy-cane-striped towers—thirty-five in all—topping the peaks that lift and separate the transmission running adjacent to the 980 acres of the valley between Blue and Wheeler Mountains.

To keep the transmission lines from swaying, at their center they are weighted with leads attached to metal counterweights that look like gigantic clothes hangers without their horizontal pants rails.

A tightly woven grid of 360 miles of copper cable conductors crisscrosses the valley below to complete this antenna system.

I'm telling you this just to point out how dangerous this is. One mistake, and you're fried alive.

And yet, this unique setup creates a mile-wide one-million-watt antenna, making it possible for our military's encoded low-frequency radio transmissions to bounce across the Pacific Ocean to the submarines that must hear them.

Command Central for all of this is a windowless cinderblock building located thirty-five feet below ground. Besides the fear of a nuclear missile attack, this protects the facility against Mother Nature's terrestrial tantrums, be they earthquakes or volcanic eruptions. Copper sheathing also shields the building from any electromagnetic field disturbances.

We're dressed casually, like campers: jeans or khakis, long tees or plaid shirts. Though it's summer, the evening is chilly enough for jackets. Baseball caps all around.

Abu hits the ground first—with an audible curse, but he rolls to safety before Arnie plops practically in the same spot. Because Evan has never skydived, he's harnessed to Jack. They land some fifty yards further down in the valley. From five stories above, I watch as the rest of my team quickly gathers their parachutes and stuffs them into rucksacks.

I'm the last to land, but the gods must be angry because an updraft makes me overshoot my mark. Worse yet, it's pulling me toward the transmission grid.

I stall my canopy just in time—

Okay, maybe I pulled up on my toggles too fast—

The right toggle, anyway, because I'm flung backward—

Smack into a grassy hillside.

The wind is knocked out of me.

I hear Jack running toward me, but I can't see him because my parachute has enveloped me, shrouding my vision.

"Breathe, Donna! Try to breathe…."

It takes me a while to gasp in the air again.

In our ears, Emma says, "Jack, stop! I see a human flare —not from any of our team—and it's coming Donna's way!"

Then Ryan: "If it's the Russian agent's contact, Donna will have to play along until we identify the individual."

"But…We don't know her alias!" Jack argues. "For that matter, we don't even know her real name!"

"She wouldn't have used her real name with him anyway," Ryan insists. "Just do it! That way, Donna can pass him the intel we want him to have instead."

Jack sighs. "Donna, don't worry. I, and the others, will be within view of you at all times."

I stay put. In time, I hear footsteps. Then:

A bird whistle.

I mimic it.

The footsteps get closer: Then: "Yelena?"

"Yes," I whisper.

His flashlight hits my face.

I hold up my hands to shield my eyes. "Stop it," I growl.

He chuckles. "I just wanted to see if you're as pretty as I imagined."

So, they haven't met, thank goodness!

"I hope I pass muster," I mutter.

He's close enough now that he looms over me. He's over six feet tall, broad-shouldered, hulking—and around my age. Although the flashlight is pointed directly at the ground, its light is bright enough to illuminate his face. Leering, Hulk murmurs, "Hell yeah, you'll do."

"Glad I have your approval."

He guffaws. "Your American accent is perfect. Well, I guess that's par for the course, what with you being a spy and all." He jerks me onto my feet. "Frankly, I thought you'd already be in the cabin, waiting for me."

I shrug. "I had a later start than anticipated. I can give you what you need right here and now."

He snickers. "That's not exactly what I envisioned when you said you like it rough. What's your rush? You're staying the night, remember? I tricked out your cabin with all kinds of goodies. Trust me, I know how to show a lady a good time." To prove it, his left hand fondles my right breast. "Can't wait to bury my head between this little lady and her twin." With his other hand, he jerks me close against his hard-on. "And as you can see, my other head is also raring to go."

I purr, "Business before pleasure."

"Sure, if that's the way you want it. I've got what you want right here." He pats his jacket pocket. "But we don't do the exchange until I see the money go into my Bahamas account."

"That means he's giving her some intel as well as embedding the Russian trojan," Ryan whispers in my ear.

"It also means that Yelena is already in the cabin he reserved for her, waiting for him to join her," Jack mutters. "Donna, you'll need to take him to our cabin instead. Make up some excuse—like, you reserved a second one in case he somehow blew his cover."

"Sure, okay," I say to Jack—though Yelena's asset thinks I'm talking to him. "But I've got a surprise for you too. I booked a different cabin… for us."

"Why'd you do that?" Hulk's annoyance is palpable.

"Because I don't leave anything to chance—including

the possibility that you haven't been as careful as you should be." I grab him below and squeeze. "See? This is a perfect example of how you've made yourself vulnerable."

Hulk grunts in pain, but he must like it because his mouth lands on mine. It's not a kiss, more of a cavity search with his tongue. "At least let me get the whipped cream out of the fridge. I'd hate to see it go to waste."

"Trust me, I've got something tastier than that. The sooner we get there, the sooner you find out what it is." I grab his hand, leading the way.

IT'S A GOOD TWENTY-MINUTE WALK TO THE CABIN: JUST LONG enough for Emma to run Hulk's facial recognition analysis through the Navy's human resources database and ID him as Officer Steve Jenkins, a CWE—that is, a cyber warfare engineer.

In other words, the perfect asset to turn. Others on the base won't suspect that their intel has been compromised.

As far as Steve's offshore account is concerned, he's sloppy enough to have accessed it on his personal computer. Even the password is easily hackable: his dog's name, his mother's birth date, and a dollar sign in between. Acme knows this because it's listed in his iPhone's address book.

Dumb, dumb, dumbass move...

Abu, Arnie, and Evan also have enough time to high-tail it to our assigned cabins. While Abu and Evan bug the one assigned to Jack and me, Arnie creates a mask of

Steve's face for Jack so that he can rendezvous with Yelena—

Who's apparently a ghost since she's not showing up in any database of known Russian spies or sparrows.

One advantage of Jack getting up close and personal with her is he can put a microdot on her.

The disadvantage is that he'll have to sleep with her to do it.

In other words, we're both in for a lousy night.

"CHA-*CHING*!" STEVE HOOTS. HE'S JUST LOOKED AT HIS BANK account. Yep, the infusion of cash is there.

At least, he thinks that's what he's looking at. His passcode got him into a dummy account meant to mirror the one he opened. If Jack does his bit (and trust me, I hate the thought of what that entails), Steve will see the money that Russia's intelligence branch, SVR, put in there.

He pulls me into his lap. I almost gag as his tongue goes down my throat. I stifle the urge to bite down to hear him yelp in pain. Instead, I stand up. "So what do you have for me?"

"I thought you'd never ask." While he stands to unzip his trousers, I slip my hand into his jacket pocket and pull out the intel instead. "I meant this, silly boy." I then toss him the SD card with BlackTech's trojan.

His pants drop to his knees when he catches it, revealing his skin flute.

That's not doing it justice. It's more like a *trombone*.

Yikes! I flinch at the thought of it getting anywhere near me.

Ain't happening.

I reach into my rucksack and pull out my spritzer of Acme Love Potion. "You're going to love this," I coo.

Before he knows it, he's gotten a whiff of it. In slow motion, he drops back onto the bed. "What…just happened?"

"I've ridden you hard and tuckered you out. But before you have the best sleep you ever had, tell me what's in the intel you just handed me."

"Just what you asked for—the SIGINT codebook for all naval subs," he murmurs.

I hear Ryan shouting through my earbud, "Emma, be ready to dummy up a different version of whatever Arnie passes forward!"

"Will do," she replies.

"What cabin did you reserve for me?" I ask next.

"Number 69." Steve smirks at this silly joke.

"And you'll upload the virus I gave you when you're back on your shift tomorrow, right?"

He nods solemnly.

"Now that you've had the best sex of your life, sleep tight until noonish."

By the time I walk out the door, he's on his stomach: spread-eagled, naked, and snoring.

I look around. Good. Arnie, Abu, and Evan took away everything left for the Acme team.

I lock the door behind me.

I GO NEXT DOOR. JACK SAYS, "GOOD WORK."

I shrug. "I'm sure you'll do just as well." I toss Evan the SD card with the SIGINT codebook while Arnie finishes molding Steve's mask on Jack's face.

Jack grimaces. "Yeah, well…different circumstances. We can't just leave her with a pleasant memory."

"No, *you* can't. But you will." I roll my eyes. "What if she's also playing honeypot with the other turned assets? There may be something about you that she'll remember."

Because of the look on my face, Jack's chuckle is half-hearted. "Then we better pray that Dominic gets out of his coma soon."

I don't laugh, and not just because it's a lousy joke.

"How was his kiss?"

"Like having a boa constrictor in my mouth." I scowl. "But you needn't follow his lead. She may actually like it. Hey, here's a thought, try to be a lousy lover. Since they've never met, she'll know he's like most men: all talk."

As if.

Fifteen minutes later, Acme relays the fake code to Evan. He uploads it onto the SD card.

Jack is out the door with it. He takes Steve's truck. Abu shadows him in the van, but he'll park it far enough away that Yelena won't know he's lurking outside her cabin in case something goes wrong.

It already has, but Jack won't admit it.

To my husband's credit, he's doing his best to make it a less than memorable assignation—

Even though Yelena meets him at the door in a short silk bathrobe tethered loosely with a sash which provides plenty of opportunities for her boobs, butt, and nether regions to play peek-a-boo. She's now blonde, with long flowing tendrils.

Jack has got Steve's tone and attitude down pat, which means he manhandles Yelena often while he verifies the payment.

She pretends to enjoy it.

Is she also faking her surprised yelp when he slams her face up against the wall and lifts her robe over her ass?

How real are her moans when he enters her from behind?

Do her legs ache when she must rise on her toes as he thrusts into her, again and again?

When he finally comes, is he truly so exhausted that he must crush her against the wall?

No, he's not faking that.

I know because he makes the same satisfied groan when he does it to me.

And as he once did with me on that first mission we shared, he's put a microdot on her.

Yelena is certainly not faking the ecstatic smile or the desire in her eyes. As Jack tosses on his clothes, she begs him to stay, promising to make it worth his while.

His answer: a deep, savage kiss. My reconnaissance paid off after all.

When he finally pulls away, she puts her arms around

his neck as if he's her lifeline. Still, he shrugs her off and heads out the door.

She watches as he drives away, then reaches into her bag, pulling out a satellite phone and a dildo.

She's reporting on the success of her mission on the former.

Then she goes to bed, bringing herself to orgasm with the latter.

A half-hour later, she's packed and gone.

Abu, who has been waiting patiently outside the cabin, jimmies the lock and enters it. Once inside, he dusts for prints. He finds a few long blond hairs in the bed and drops them in a vial.

Her panties are tangled in her bedsheet. Abu takes them too. Maybe the DNA will be a match to some ally's database.

9

Play Games, All Sorts!

THESE DAYS, PARTY GAMES ARE ALL THE RAGE! TO JUMPSTART your soirée before it's deemed DOA, consider these wild and crazy conversation starters:

*1: **Make it tactile.** Keeping things touchy-feely is a wonderful way to keep your guests loosie-goosie. That's not to say you should encourage some slap-and-tickle. However, a limber crowd mukes for a happy one. You say you dumped your Twister mat after it put your hubby in traction? Perhaps go for something simpler, like the "Pass the Orange" game. It's one way to gauge the dexterity of those you may need to wrestle to the ground when, inevitably, things get out of hand.*

***2: Keep it simple, stupid!** Trivia? Don't pursue it. Memory games? No need to embarrass those who aren't the sharpest tools in the shed. If you shame them, they'll pass on your next invitation. Unless you want to play Solitaire the rest of your life, make it a game where everyone gets a trophy. (How Millennial, right?)*

3: Final bit of advice: Don't believe your hubby when he

tells you kissing games are back in vogue. *Whether he's waxing nostalgic about his middle school years or he's got the hots for the neighborhood slut, hold your ground that no one shall be playing Spin the Bottle or Seven Minutes in Heaven. If you have to make your point the hard way, coerce him to allow you to blindfold him, lock him in the basement, and leave him there.*

Then move to a different town.

In a week or two, he'll get the message.

WE'RE ABOUT TO LAND IN GREAT FALLS, MONTANA, WHEN Emma calls: "Yelena got to Malmstrom AFB half hour ago. She checked into the on-base hotel, Malmstrom Inn & Suites. I've booked three rooms there: one beside her first floor 'distinguished visitor' suite, and the other two in a different building."

"Donna, you and Jack are to take one in the other building," Ryan informs us.

"No shit," I mutter.

I ignore Jack's frown. I cold-shouldered him the entire flight. I know he's only doing his job. I just hate that he does it so well.

And too often.

With others.

"I'm sure we're of like minds, Mrs. Craig, as to why I even brought it up," Ryan adds.

Doubtful. But sure, I'll play along: "Of course, sir! But do tell since I hate coming off as the teacher's pet."

"There's no chance of that today," he huffs. "Since it's not so obvious, let me assure you that the reason is simple enough: if Yelena were to run into Jack—or you—and recognize something, it could hurt the mission."

Before retorting with something I'd later regret—like, maybe pointing out that I won't be wearing my red pig-tailed wig and cat-eye glasses and Jack won't be walking around the lodge naked, so it may be a moot point—Jack asks, "What's Yelena's cover?"

"She checked in as Deborah Connelly, a wine representative with Rasputin Vodka."

Arnie guffaws. "Talk about keeping it in the 'hood. *Prost!*"

"Hmmm…." We can hear Emma clicking away on her computer. "In fact, Rasputin Vodka supplies almost every US military base."

I sneer. "Well, now, isn't that convenient?"

"I'll check into Rasputin's incorporation and who approved the contract for it to provide booze for the bases," Emma declares.

"Now that Yelena has her room assignment, Emma's ComInt team has hacked into its WiFi signal," Ryan informs us. "Thus far, 'Deborah' has only used it to confirm today's appointments with the managers of both of the base's liquor-serving restaurants—the Elkhorn Diner and the one in its bowling alley."

"All places where brush passes can take place," I reason. "And let's not forget the hotel too."

"Four possible drop locations—and four of us," Evan

points out. "I guess each of us needs to stake out one of them."

"Not necessary," I counter. "You're forgetting that Jack successfully planted the tracking microdot on her."

Evan turns bright red.

My husband grimaces. "Guilty as charged."

"Not at all," Ryan declares. "You came through with flying colors."

Now I'm pinking up—

Really, my anger must be turning my face purple because I feel it heating up.

Calm…down…

"Speaking of Acme's Love Potion, our operatives' field research has turned up some pretty interesting anomalies—"

"'*Field research?*" I snort. "Is that what you call it! Well, this ought to be good!"

"Mrs. Craig, you may find these statistics interesting, considering the recent failure with your last attempt to use it—not to mention Dominic's outcome with it."

Okay, yeah, he's shut me up.

"It's been used over a hundred times each by male and female operatives. Whereas its success rate by our female operatives is over eighty-two percent—with failures when used in windy or non-contained spaces —its success rate among male operatives comes in very low: just thirty-one percent. As for our male operatives, its aftermath was less than desirable even in those cases where it worked. The targets were warier. Also, they were more reluctant to give the intel asked. A few even fought off our operatives' attempts."

"Any idea why the ladies aren't loving it?" Arnie asks.

"We broached that very question to our scientists," Ryan replies. "Their theory is that the serum works so great on men because they're in a pheromonal state before sex, therefore more likely to be in an emotionally susceptible state afterward. Additionally, their minds have already put their bodies in an anticipatory mode for it—like a trance, or self-hypnosis."

Oy. I roll my eyes. "Go on."

"On the other hand, in anticipation of sex, women's senses are heightened. Ergo, unlike males, when the drug is used on them, the memories are pleasant, sure…but they also realize that something isn't quite natural about the experience," Ryan explains. "Apparently, for women, sex is more of a—well, I guess you'd call it an emotional experience. When the Acme Love Potion's hypnotic effect wears off, they are left anxious. As you'd imagine, the memory gaps concern them. They actually worry if they were drugged. Not surprisingly, this reaction was more consistently reported by those whose pasts include sexual abuse or rape. Doubly so if previous incidents—crimes— occurred when the subject had first been given Rohypnol."

"Understandable," I admit. "And if you're in diplomatic intelligence or some other highly competitive profession, chances are you're weighing all come-ons with that mindset to begin with."

In other words, the men are getting a pass on using it.

Figures.

Pointedly, Jack looks at me and shrugs his shoulders.

"The turned asset has made contact with 'Deborah!'" Emma's excitement is palpable. "They're meeting at the bowling alley tonight after her last appointment." Her fingers move at lightning speed on her computer's keyboard: "He's reserved two lanes: Number Eight for himself and Number Nine for 'Debbie Doo.' Quote-unquote: 'We'll hook up at eight o'clock.'"

"Of course, they are," I mutter.

Jack sighs.

"She sent back a kiss emoji," Emma continues. "He's calling from a burner phone which he's also used for a couple of porn accounts. They're attached to a credit card assigned to the name 'Phil Carlisle.'" A few clicks later, she adds: "I've got him ID'ed in the Navy's personnel data-base. Like Steve, he's a cyber warfare engineer."

A photo of Phil appears on the monitor: tall, good-looking, square-jawed, All-American, and a ginger.

"I see a pattern here," Arnie pipes up.

Duh.

Lucky lady. Thus far, her targets have been Princes Charming as opposed to toads.

Ryan chuckles. "I've just had a brilliant idea! Emma, block his calls to her and hers to him until she's out of the area. Phil texts back that he has to move their rendezvous up by ninety minutes because he'll be called back onto his shift later tonight. That way, Jack can intercept it as Phil, and Evan can analyze Phil's SD card. Afterward, Donna can pass the real Phil the card with the altered algorithm."

Great. Just…great.

As the Soviet Slut, I'm throwing a few gutter balls whereas Jack will be doing yet another horizontal rhumba with the real deal.

"Because of Jack's previous reconnaissance, I've got enough video footage of 'Debbie Doo' to build Donna's mask," Abu assures us. "As soon as Emma can scrounge up some of Phil, I'll build out Jack's too."

"On it," Emma exclaims.

"You've got your marching orders, people." Before the monitor goes dark, Ryan gives us a thumbs up.

Jack pats my arm. "Sorry, babe."

"Don't be. All in a day's work, right?" I nod at Abu. "Depending on Morton's staying power, Jack may be bunking with you for the evening."

Jack's jaw drops. "Ah! I... I assumed you'll drop the intel and be out of there."

"Funny, now that you slapped that microdot on Yelena, I assumed the same about you. I guess we're both wrong to presume anything—especially since he's got such a cute nickname for 'Debbie Doo'—*and* he's expecting a quote-unquote hook-up."

"I don't think he meant it literally."

I giggle. "I guess I'll find out soon enough."

Now, I'm the one who's getting the silent treatment until our plane's wheels skid onto the tarmac.

Suddenly, I feel like the dog who caught the car.

I'm taking my vial of Acme's Love Potion with me.

Not that Jack has to know this.

~

ABU'S MASK AND MAKEUP MAGIC WORK AGAIN: JACK IS A dead ringer for Phil Jenkins, down to the khaki-colored tee-shirt that strains against his broad back and rock-hard biceps and the worn jeans that hug his thighs.

After Jack walks out the door, Arnie, Evan, and I scan the base's webcam feed between the hotel and the bowling alley.

It's a slow night. The only lanes being used are toward the front of the alley. In fact, no one hovers around our lanes at the far end of the entrance—

Except for Abu, who works a broom on the floor behind the lanes.

By the time Yelena-slash-Debbie Doo gets there, Jack has already scored two strikes. He glances over at her and nods just slightly enough for it to pass as a crick in the neck. The facility's security cameras won't pick it up because Arnie has them looped with footage from the past hour.

Yelena responds by licking her lips, which puts the ghost of a smile on Jack's mug before he takes a running shot:

It's a spare.

It should convince her that just seeing her has thrown him off his game.

I do not doubt that this is the case.

Yelena saunters by him to the next lane but takes her time putting on her bowling shoes. Though Jack tries not to stare, his smirk signals his pleasure in watching the dainty way she slips on her snug, slim bowling gloves: black, with the tallest and fourth fingers cut off after the first knuckle. The thumbs aren't sheathed, but the opening is piped in the bright cherry red that matches her blouse and short pleated skirt.

Jack gives her the courtesy of waiting for her to take her shot. I'm sure he likes what he sees: not just the fact that she lines up with her lane perfectly for hitting the pocket, but also how she bends and extends herself, right leg out behind her, back arched just so, before releasing the ball—

Strike!

Excitedly she squeals, bounces, stretches sensually—

Then falls back onto the bench.

By the time her bowling ball returns to her, she's placed a matchbox on the flat rail of the seat that separates her lane from Jack's.

The matchbox is gone when she returns.

Jack is already packing up to leave. A moment later, he walks out of the building.

Yelena pouts, disappointed.

I assume she was expecting him to be another of her conquests.

In no time, he's back in the hotel room. He hands the SD card to Evan, who begins analyzing the algorithms and then modifying the code with the trojan.

In the meantime, Jack takes the chair beside mine.

I can't resist: "So…that's it?"

"I assume it's a straight business proposition with Phil." To make his point, he shows me what else was in the matchbox—a tiny slip of paper:

32-15-39 / 24

"What is it?"

"The combination and cubby number in the bowling alley's locker room," Jack replies. "Inside was a bowling bag filled with cash. I left it for the real Phil Jenkins to find when you give him this." He hands me the matchbox.

Together we watch as Yelena packs up her ball, changes out of her shoes, and leaves.

Abu waits until she's out the door before taking off.

A moment later, he's in the room too. He's got a bowling bag with him, from which he pulls a ball, gloves, and shoes.

"Oooh, presents!" I coo.

"Consider it an early Christmas gift." Abu nods in the direction of the chair in front of the mirror. "Ready for your close-up?"

I allow Phil a good quarter-hour lead before arriving at the bowling alley. He ignores me as I settle into my lane.

He's a power player. The ball gets a big wind-up before he plants, pulls hard, and lets go of his ball.

I'm struck by the memory of Yelena's lust-filled eyes at Jack. And she wasn't Phil's type?

Strange.

My bowling antics aren't as salaciously silly as Yelena's. Phil isn't watching anyway. I guess he's figured out that the last thing he needs is to get caught in a treasonous act.

While waiting for my ball to return, I follow Yelena's lead and leave the matchbox on top of the rail.

Afterward, I throw a few more balls: a strike, a spare, a split, and then another split.

Ah, well. I guess it's fate's way of telling me it's time to get outta here.

Phil has beaten me to the punch. He's already packed up and gone—

Toward the locker room anyway.

I change shoes, put away the rest of my gear, and head out the door.

I'M HALFWAY TO THE LODGE WHEN I REALIZE THAT MEN ARE now flanking me closely on both sides. I stop cold, only to bump into another one who apparently has been trailing behind me. "What is this, anyway?"

The guy on my right practically shouts: "FBI! Deborah Connelly, you're under arrest for the act of Espionage. Get on your knees and put your hands on your head—*now*! Do it!"

Slowly, I lift my arms. "Woah, woah—"

The next thing I know, I'm face down on the asphalt.

As I'm read my rights, I hear Phil's voice behind me: "Here's the evidence, sir."

I try turning my head to see who Phil is talking to. But

the oaf who has his foot on my back also has a gun to my head.

Jack is saying, "Excuse me, gentlemen, but I think you'll want to take this call from Director of National Intelligence Marcus C. Branham—"

The angle of my head allows me to see a car roll up to the guard station:

Yelena is in the driver's seat, oblivious to this circus in which I, her doppelgänger, has the starring role as Clown on the Ground.

Make that Suspect in Custody.

She's waved through. Off she goes.

"I'M SO SORRY, MA'AM." PHIL IS GENUINELY CONTRITE. "I swear, you can be Debbie Doo's spitting image."

"Yeah, well, that was the goal." I shrug. "And to be honest, I'm heartened that you aren't actually a traitor."

Phil chuckles, as does his commanding officer, Colonel Helen Raymond, who insists: "He's the biggest eagle scout on the base. When Connolly approached him, he let us know immediately. Of course, we contacted the closest FBI office and informed the assigned agents of the offer she made to Phil"— she rolls her eyes — "both of them."

"I turned down the other so that she couldn't claim entrapment," Phil is quick to say.

"And now that DNI Branham has explained the situation, you realize the importance of our counter-intelligence operation continuing as planned?" I ask.

"Yes, of course!" Colonel Raymond insists. "Although Officer Jenkins and I are only on a 'need to know' basis, we understand why we shouldn't disrupt your mission."

"We're sorry we couldn't loop you in on it, but as DNI Branham explained, the issue is sensitive," Jack adds. "Had the operative left even five minutes later, our mission would have been blown sky high."

"Not to worry. I'll do exactly what DNI Branham requested: upload the data—and keep my mouth shut about it." Phil nods goodbye before taking off.

His commanding officer is right on his heels.

"All's well that ends well," Jack declares.

"I'm sure Yelena was wondering why Phil never fell for her come-ons."

"She tried hard enough," he admits.

Here's hoping she won't succeed next time.

10

The Gracious Hostess Test

I ask you now: could you pass The Gracious Hostess Test?"

"How hard can it be?" you reply (smugly, I might add).

Okay, here goes! All questions are true-or-false:

Question 1: For those few hours during her party, a gracious hostess always puts her guests above everything else. *(Because let's face it: throwing a soirée means putting everything else in your life on hold.)*

Question 2: A gracious hostess's priorities go in this order: *(a) Guest List (b) Menu (c) Theme and Ambiance (d) Exit Strategy (Got the local fire department on speed-dial? Yep? That's my gal!)*

Question 3: When all is said and done, what you'll cherish most are the memories of your success! *(Especially if no one got blown up, maimed, or killed.)*

If you answered "True" to all of this, congratulations! You're a great hostess indeed!

We have four and a half hours in the air before landing at North Dakota's Minot Air Force Base.

"The microdot tracker shows that we're just two hours behind Yelena," Ryan informs us. Having intercepted the texts between her and Phil and the frequency of her satellite hotline to Moscow, we can track her messaging. This time, the asset she's turned isn't on the base. Jack and Donna, you'll be shadowing her separately. One of you will partner with Evan, the other with Arnie, in case her object is an SD card brush pass."

"Are you assuming that it may be something else?" I ask.

"Hard to tell," Emma explains. "It's odd that none of her coded messages are going to the base's CWEs. Instead, she's using a burner phone and texting under the name of 'Janet Morris' to about sixty civilians in the area. They are all married women and range in age from twenty to forty. We're doing a cross-check now to see their relationship to each other."

"What's the message she's sent out?" I ask.

"'See you today at the party,' exclamation point. 'I've got your goodies and a special gift,' again with the exclamation point." Emma sniffs. "It's the most over-used punctuation in our language; thank you very much, the son of a bitch who invented texting."

"I think you're wrong," I insist. "As with the end of the proper salutation, it started with damned email—"

"Nope. It goes back even further," Abu interjects. "We

should blame the bastard who created the exclamation point, back in the eighteen-twenties—"

"Stay on point, people!" Ryan bellows.

"If I may, boss, and trust me when I tell you I'm still on point: Could that—not just the exclamation point, but the whole message—be part of a code for the time and place of some sort of liaison?" Jack wonders out loud.

"And if so, does that mean she'll be doing individual brush-passes with each woman?" Abu adds.

"By looking at the text thread with these women, which goes on for a month, I don't think she'll have to. Whatever she's doing, it'll be done in plain sight," Emma replies.

"Don't keep us in suspense," Ryan growls.

"What I'm trying to say is that there *is* no hidden message," Emma insists. "'Janet Morris' is the regional Supperware representative."

"You mean to say she goes door to door selling plastic housewares to these women?" Jack asks.

"No, silly. Someone hosts the party at their home," I explain. "And the hostess gets her items for free as well as a commission."

"The local hostess is someone named Isabel Weber." Emma's next pause comes with a few clicks, followed by a low whistle. "Apparently, Supperware is *big* here. 'Janet' is hauling in some cash! Check out the 'Top Sellers' list on the company's website. She's, like, number eight in the country."

What she sees on her screen now appears on our plane's TV monitor.

Abu's draw drops open. "Sheesh, Emma's right." He taps me on my arm. "Hey, we should get in on this action."

I guffaw. "Yeah, sure. In my spare time."

"So, what's the common denominator among the guests?" Jack wonders.

"Oh…my…God! I think I found it," Emma exclaims. Her voice trails off. "They're either spouses or significant others of pilots who fly for the base's Bomb Wing—that is, the 740th, 741st, and 742nd Missile Squadrons or its Missile Wing."

"The 91st, which is one of only three in the US Air Force," Jack points out.

"In other words, these women are as close as you can get to the pilots who'll be flying Minute Men Missile IIIs or the service personnel with their fingers on the button," Evan points out.

"Donna will have to infiltrate the party," Ryan declares.

"There are sixty women on the guest list. I'll go through it and see who's the best fit for her to take their place." Emma's keyboard taps are proof she's started the process.

Evan grimaces. "The woman is sure to have friends who may think she's not exactly acting herself."

"Acme arranges for the target to have a stomach bug," Arnie explains. "Trust me, what comes out of both ends ain't pretty, but it does the trick of keeping them down for the count for at least forty-eight hours."

Evan's jaw drops.

"I may have come across a possible match," Emma replies. A photo appears on the screen: buxom, apple-cheeked, freckles, blond curly hair. She's wearing a dress too tight and too short. "Mitzi Finnegan is new to the base. She's the wife of James Patrick Finnegan—known as Jimmy—who flies for the 742nd Missile Squadron. They just moved into their place last week."

"Then she should be new to the other attendees," I reason. "Why won't she be at the party?"

"According to the text she sent Isabel—who has yet to see it and now won't, since I'm wiping it from her cell—Mitzi had to go out of town to be with Jimmy's mom while she's undergoing knee surgery."

"How soon will we know what Yelena-slash-Janet is passing and to whom?" Jack asks.

"Thus far, except for the one group email about the upcoming party, Yelena has only been corresponding with Isabel."

"Perhaps you should also scan the products ordered by the attendees," I suggest. "If someone has ordered something that none of the others have on their list, maybe that item will contain the intel being passed to Yelena's turned asset."

"Great idea," Emma replies.

"The Supperware party is a brunch, scheduled for ten-thirty this morning," Ryan informs us. "Better get some shut-eye, folks."

"You're still mad at me—about Yelena." Jack isn't asking a question.

He's figured out the obvious. We may be lying in the same bed, but that's all.

I sit up. "You're right. Sorry. I know it's what we have to do. You've chosen to do it, and I have to live with your decision. So be it."

Now he's back up too. "Do you think I enjoy screwing the enemy?"

"If you don't, you certainly give a great impression of it." I clap my hands. "Oscar! Oscar!"

"That's not fair," he huffs. "Look, I hold it together every time you play the honey pot. Do you think I find that easy?"

"Apparently, screwing Yelena's brains out was easier than giving her Acme's truth serum."

"You heard Ryan. Even if research on the love potion hadn't come up with those findings, it wasn't the right place or time to use it," Jack argues. "Too much could have gone wrong. You and I both know that."

"You've never even given it a try," I counter. "It was the same on our last two missions: with Hansley Bardot, and before that, with Theodora Lawton."

"And I told you why then. I'll reiterate it now: the stakes are too high to trust it to a spray that can—and has—failed us. Have you forgotten how quickly that lounge lizard, Richard Seymour, broke out of his fog?"

Jack has got a point. The stuff isn't failsafe.

He puts his head next to mine. "Donna, you know as well as I do that using our bodies to coerce others to tell us what we need to know—it's...it's *what we do*. Neither of us likes it. Neither of us wants to do it. But it's a necessary evil."

"As long as we're with Acme…" I don't have to finish my sentence.

Jack kisses me. "Just say the word."

I stay silent.

Instead, I show him.

It starts with my mouth on his. Soon my tongue is roaming across his body, hungry for what I am genuinely missing: the taste of his skin on my lips—neck, chest, shoulder, stomach, hips—

And yes, his cock: hard and thick, slick with anticipation of how it will feel inside me.

Why prolong the pleasure? Why not just submit to the ecstasy?

Because Jack won't let me.

It's not what he says but what he does.

With a quick flip, now he's on top, his lips ravishing mine. Before I know it, he holds both my wrists on the pillow above my head with his left arm. A finger on his right roams from my forehead to the tip of my nose, then to my lips. I suck hard, eliciting a groan from him.

Good. He's been teasing me. It's time for me to taunt him.

I rise up, breasts to chest. Surprised, he eases back onto the bed. Fully erect now, he enters me.

The dance begins as a tango; flesh upon flesh, each move anticipated, then mirrored by your partner. In time, it becomes a rage: a mindless, frenzied free-for-all that leaves you spent, sopping—

Euphoric.

Five minutes later, my heart is still racing.

Jack, exhausted, is fast asleep.

Just as the survey says.

How can I explain to him that no other woman should be left with the memory of his touch, of his taste?

Certainly not those we revile.

Just me.

Only and always.

IN CASE ANYONE IS WATCHING, I WALK OUT OF MITZI Finnegan's house, which is currently unattended. Most of their belongings are still boxed up since she is with Jimmy's mother, and Jimmy is at flight training school for the week.

Isabel Weber's home is the right side of a tidy two-story duplex that mirrors its twin almost exactly in its shiny white coat of paint, begonia-bedecked planters, and the two late-model cars in the driveway.

One of them has a rental car sticker.

Yelena's, I assume.

Evan, Arnie, Abu, and Jack are in the back of a van parked in front of the next duplex. It's plastered with the logo of the region's internet company.

"Can you hear us?" Arnie asks.

I reach down and straighten the strap on my heel to prove I can.

"Cute," Jack murmurs.

"You too," I mutter back.

My team is laughing now.

In my purse is a keychain tethered to a miniature Magic Eight Ball. I'll leave it somewhere innocuous and yet within proximity of Yelena. If my contact lenses miss anything, the rest of the team may still pick it up.

Isabel's front door has been left wide open. I'm greeted by a cacophony of gossip and giggles from those attending the event. On purpose, I'm the last to enter. In fact, our host, Isabel Weber, has just walked back into the foyer to close the door. Seeing me, her eyes don't immediately register recognition. Why should it? She only knows Mitzi via the base's weekly family email, which announces its local events, school missives, and new move-ins.

After introducing myself, she exclaims, "It's so great to finally meet you—and for you to make it on such short notice!" Isabel air-kisses me on both sides of my face. "After the presentation, I'll introduce you around to everyone. And while I know you'll just want to tear through the catalog and buy a lot of wonderful doodads, I understand you've just moved in, so no pressure! Besides, everyone walks out with a free Supperware gift anyway! And this one is extra special!"

"How nice," I reply. I guess I could show a little more enthusiasm, but in a million years, I couldn't match Isabel's bright-eyed cheer squad-worthy gushing, so why even try?

Besides, I want her to forget I was even here.

There aren't enough seats to go around, so like many others, I've propped myself against a wall in Isabel's spacious combination living room-slash-dining room. Yelena stands dead center of both rooms next to a side table laden with white, beige, gray, and black samples of the latest and greatest in Supperware products. She's brunette today. Her hair is swept up in a chignon. Her suit is boxy enough to hide her svelte figure.

"Donna," Jack says in my ear: "The upright piano that's against the wall, with all the family pictures on its top: what say you leave the Magic Eight Ball there?"

He's right. If I lay it right on top, it's tall enough to take in the whole length of the room.

"On it," I whisper.

Slowly, I make my way over. I've just slipped the key ring in front of a photograph of one of Isabel's boys winding up for a pitch and have sat down on the piano bench when I notice that Yelena is looking my way.

I lean forward a bit, feigning interest in what she's saying.

"—And this year, you'll note that the theme is elegance, regarding Supperware's latest color palette and its sleeker product designs. But of course, it still has Supperware's patented load-and-lock seal-tight guarantee." Yelena picks up one of the plastic pieces—the size and dimensions of a typical sandwich—and opens its lid with a resounding pop. It contains a serving of pasta with a red sauce. "Here's the ultimate proof that you'll rest assured that even a single serving of last night's spaghetti is safely secured."

Then fast and furiously, she flings it at me—

I duck as it sails over my head.

The women squeal as Yelena's projectile slams hard, like a discus, into the pale green accent wall behind me, right between portraits of Isabel and her husband, Henry, before ricocheting onto the floor.

The women's gasps fill the room.

All eyes go to Isabel. At first, she blanches, but then her eyes narrow into angry slits. Her smile has hardened from sunshine to stone.

Yelena saunters over, picks it up, and opens it. Then, scanning the room to assure that all eyes are on her—

She flips it over.

A chorus of gasps fills the room—

Until the women realize that the food has stayed inside the container.

Yelena holds it out vertically so the attendees can see why: a thin plastic film is still securing its contents. "Supperware's scientists have added a new innovation! We call it the 'Take No Chances' screen. With a mere tap"—she makes her point with a cherry-lacquered nail — "you can now add an extra layer of seal-tight freshness to all your stored foods."

Her pronouncement is met with cheers and applause.

Isabel forces a smile onto her beet-red face.

One woman exclaims, "Oh my god! Where do we sign up?"

"All our newest offerings and tried-and-true favorites are laid out for you here. Just point at the QR Code with your phone, and it will be placed in your online cart." Yelena points to the dining room table. Then, reaching into one of its chair seats, she pulls out a tiny gift bag. "And for all who attended today, we've got an exceptional gift!" A tiny jewel box is inside. She opens it revealing a solid silver rectangle.

She holds it up. A photo of Isabel, Henry, and their two boys is imprinted on one side. Handing it to the closest woman to pass around, Yelena adds, "Each bag here has one of your names on it. Enclosed you'll find this sterling silver commemorative dog tag embossed with your family photo. If you remember, you were offered a free family portrait last month. Supperware underwrote it to say thanks for your ongoing appreciation of our products."

The women ooh and ahh.

"Here's hoping they wear it always, when and wherever they serve their country."

Applause reverberates through the room. Some women are so touched that they get up to give "Janet" a group hug.

The next thing I know, Isabel is beside me. She hands me a Supperware bag. "I'm sorry that you weren't already on the base when the photos were taken. So that you weren't left out, I hope you don't mind that I gave Janet the photo you posted on Facebook that was taken at your wedding."

"Oh… *My goodness*! Thank you!" I embrace her tightly. "I must go now. Jimmy's mom has knee surgery tomorrow, and I have a long drive ahead of me."

"Why, of course! Godspeed!" Isabel shoos me out.

While walking back to Mitzi's house, I pass my mission team's van. The front passenger window is open. I toss the gift bag through it.

"So, right," Abu mutters.

When I reach my car, the van has already driven away. Through my earbuds, I hear Arnie crowing, "Evan—*for real*? If what you say is true… Jesus, Mary, and Joseph—*it's the golden ticket!*"

"Quit speaking in tongues," I warn him.

"We'll explain when we get back to the plane," Jack adds.

I can't wait to hear what Yelena did this time.

EVERYONE IS ON ACME'S PLANE EXCEPT FOR ARNIE. BEFORE I can ask where he is, Abu motions to the monitor, which shows Ryan and Marcus on a split screen.

Marcus is saying: "Jack, if I understand you correctly, you want me to tell the base commander to request that the service personnel who received the photographic dog tags from their spouses turn the tags over to him so that he can personalize them with his own inscription?"

"Yes, sir," Jack replies.

"Truly a head-scratcher," Marcus grumbles.

"I'm sure you can make it sound legitimate," Jack insists, "and for a good reason. According to our technical analysis team, the tags are tracking devices that will collect flight data from the pilots. It also has a frequency that will jamb the release of the payload, which would cause a mid-air implosion."

"The pilots will be sitting ducks," Ryan reasons.

"Exactly," Jack insists. "Furthermore, the scenario for

military personnel within the silo launch facilities is just as dire. Their tags can jamb a launch or transmit the launch's coordinates coded through its signal."

Stunned, Ryan and Marcus stare out at us. Finally, Marcus replies, "I assume the order to confiscate the tags should be immediate."

"Yes, sir. One of our tech crew, Arnie, is still at the base. Now that we've broken the algorithm on one of the tags, Evan is sending him the necessary code adjustment. That way, it and the other fifty-nine tags will allow us to forward misleading intel, per DNI Branham's instructions."

"Godspeed." That one word from Marcus expresses the gravity felt by us all.

When he disappears from the screen, we're left staring at Ryan.

"Great work, folks." He pauses. "Emma is reading Yelena's burner cell messages. Thus far, there have been no texts regarding her brush pass. I don't know what our Russian spy has in store for us next, but at the very least, she and her handlers have been ingenious in their methods of sabotage."

The screen goes blank.

"We'll be landing at Warren Air Force Base in less than four hours. How long will it take for Arnie to complete his assignment and join us in Cheyenne?" I ask.

Evan shrugs. "I'll be up the rest of the night sending Arnie unique replacement codes for each tag. New transmitters will be placed in identical dog tags created with the photos we hacked from the local photographer who took the military couples' portraits and the AF motto. The base commander has already complimented the tags to his troops' spouses and requested they be turned over immediately so that he can add his own salutation. He'll have Arnie flown to Warren AFB after he's made the changes."

I give Evan a hug. "I'm glad you're here."

His smile is bittersweet. "I feel the same way about you."

Is he thinking of Mary?

I know I am. "If she knew, Mary would be proud of you."

"I think so." He shrugs modestly. "I can't wait to see her next to tell her about it."

I wonder how she'll take the news: first, that he's out in the field with us, and secondly, that he's working around the clock in a perilous situation.

I'd expect she'd be concerned.

Will she also be envious?

$$11$$

How to Make Your Party a Blowout

Everyone wants their soirée to be the social event of *the season! Admit it: even you!*

To ensure that it's the invitation everyone is waiting for, do the following;

Set the scene with a theme! "Carnivale," you say? LOVE IT!

First, make the food fit the mood! Go big, go bold! Gourmet hot dogs, barbecue turkey legs, and waffle cheese fries will put everyone in a festive mood. You say cotton candy and candied apples for dessert? Now you're talking! Just make sure to include a no-liability clause on the RSVP that is returned by your guests. No need to spend your retirement money on someone else's dental work.

Next, hire the band! By that, I don't mean an organ grinder and a monkey. (Trust me on this.) I'm thinking a small trio, which will keep the conversation animated—

As long as they're not wailing heavy metal ditties at the top of their lungs.

And finally, hire those who will make it a festival for the eyes, ears, and mind. Jugglers? Most definitely! So you lose a vase or two. No biggy. Aerialists? Indubitably—especially if your chandeliers are bolted tightly to steel!

Fire eaters? Hmmm. Considering the number of flammables involved, I'd pass—

Unless you're looking for an insurance payout. If so, pass around the sparklers and pray that the fire department is far enough away that your party is (in every sense of the word) a blowout.

IN CASE THERE'S BEEN A CHANGE IN HER ITINERARY, WE STILL have to wait for Yelena to leave Isabel's house and for her plane to take off first, and then shadow its course—but from far enough away that her pilot doesn't pick up our tail.

By the time we reach Cheyenne, it's the wee small hours of the morning. Whereas Jack, Abu and I have taken naps, Evan pulled an all-nighter feeding Arnie the algorithms he needs to make the necessary changes to the sixty sets of commemorative dog tags.

Before he hits the sack, he tells us that transmission to Yelena's satellite phone has been nil, so she too must have used the time to sleep.

Abu nudges us awake about seven in the morning. "George woke me to say that Emma and Ryan need to speak to us. Since Evan is sacked out in the main cabin, let's take it in here."

"Are we at Warren AFB?" Jack mutters.

"No. We followed Yelena's plane to its destination: Laramie Regional Airport. She grabbed a car and headed north."

Yawning, I motion my approval for him to click on the monitor to Acme's secure channel.

Once Ryan's face appears, he doesn't waste any time: "From what we can tell, Yelena has had absolutely no contact with anyone connected to the base: not with service personnel or their families. However, five minutes ago she communicated via text to someone on a burner phone. Emma has mapped the coordinates of the signal: a cattle ranch just north of the town of Albin and south of La Grange."

A live video feed appears on the screen: the land is essentially arid. In the distance are mountains. A ranch snuggles against a few scruffy pines and a wide stream being fed by runoff from the mountain behind it. A large herd of cows are beside it, munching on the grass.

"Who owns the land?" I ask.

A couple named Augusta and Frank Nickerson," Emma replies. "It seems the text was to Augusta. "All it says is 'Book is being returned today.'"

"In other words, Yelena, will be making a dead drop," Abu says.

Two pictures appear on the monitor. Both the man and the woman are in their early forties. Her face is lined and freckled. Frank's is sunburned and weathered despite the ten-gallon hat on his head. Augusta wears her long hair in a single braid. Silver strands are sprinkled liberally among the gold.

"The Nickersons' cattle farm has been in Frank's family for four generations," Emma tells us. "It's their sole source of income. They met in college, married young—at nineteen, in fact. Their sole child, a son, is away at college. They're considered pillars of the community. She chairs the local library's fundraisers. He's been president of the local cattlemen's association at least three times in as many decades."

"So, what would be the connection between them and Yelena?" Abu wonders.

"Maybe she made Augusta a financial offer she couldn't refuse," Jack reasons.

"Or maybe it's fear," Emma counters.

The monitor now shows an aerial view of a concrete pad surrounded by a large fence.

"I imagine it can't be easy living next to a nuclear launch silo. Their land sits adjacent to one of Warren AFB's two-person LCC's—that is launch command and control facilities," she adds. "In fact, back in the early nineteen-fifties, it was Frank's grandfather who sold the one-mile-square property to the Department of Defense."

"In other words, Frank has been living next door to a very grave threat of nuclear annihilation his whole life," Abu says.

"For Augusta, twenty-one years is a long time to be fretting about it—not only for herself but for their son, who'll inherit the ranch," I point out. "Frankly, it would unnerve me, too."

"I don't get it. How would aiding and abetting the enemy make it any less of a threat?" Jack argues.

"We don't know what exactly Yelena told Augusta to gain her sympathy," I reply.

"Exactly," Ryan adds. "No matter how Yelena got her onboard, we can't let Augusta stand in our way of keeping Yelena and her Russian handlers from carrying out our mission—which is to make them think they've carried out theirs. First, you'll allow Augusta to retrieve the item. Then, you'll track her every move to see what she does with it."

"We hear you, boss," Jack says. "In other words, shadow her until we can intercept it, analyze it, and then alter it to suit our mission's subterfuge."

"I'll let loose a couple of the SNAGs that Acme developed. That way, we can track Augusta without her knowing," Abu adds. "Evan can guide them remotely."

"Great idea. Get to it, folks." Ryan's screen goes black.

"I hate to sound ignorant, but what exactly is a "snag?" I ask.

Jack tweaks my nose. "If you'd read the Acme Innovations newsletter, you'd know."

"Sorry," I sniff. "It's just not as gripping as the latest Chris Pavone novel."

"It's just a fancy acronym for 'stereotyped nature-inspired aerial graspers.' In other words, a drone that can pass as a bird—in this case, a raven," Abu explains. "The motor is actually working wings, which make it quieter than the typical drone, allowing it to track a non-suspecting human. We'll place one outside of Augusta's house so that it can follow her to the drop location, and to where she goes afterward. It's also 'host' to a couple of meta-critters—that is, smaller drones, the size of large beetles, which can climb walls. That way we have eyes and ears when she goes inside a space where the larger SNAG would be too obvious. I better grab them and take off." He nods at Evan. "Wake Sleeping Beauty. He'll need to be up and at'em in order to man the SNAGs' controls."

In a moment he's out the door.

Ten minutes later, we shake Evan awake. After he's washed some of the weariness from his face, we head for our unmarked van.

WE'RE A HALF-HOUR BEHIND ABU WHEN ONE OF THE SNAGs relays a visual of the Nickerson homestead. In the distance, Frank is on horseback, moving cattle. Apparently, Augusta hasn't left the house.

An hour goes by when Abu's truck flies past us. He nods but keeps driving.

Our cells show Augusta leaving her house. She hops into one of the trucks parked in the driveway.

Emma confirms, "She's been given instructions via cell and is heading out."

"I'm tracking her via the raven SNAG," Abu responds. "I've slowed up so that when she passes me, I can release one of the smaller SNAGs. I'll then turn into the gas station a mile up the road."

"We'll be shadowing her from behind," Jack assures him.

"Make it a long tail," Abu suggests. "If need be, we'll play leapfrog."

His idea is sound. As desolate as the roads are out here, he'll have to keep a good distance from her so as not to raise her suspicions. I imagine Augusta is already nervous about her task at hand.

Evan maneuvers the raven SNAG so that we can see what happens as Abu passes Augusta:

Something small flies out of the bed of his truck and into hers. When it attaches itself to her rear windshield, we can watch and hear her as she texts via voice command to her cell:

Will be there in ten, then I'll drop the item.

I guess we'll soon find out what that means.

A mile down the road, Abu pulls into a gas station and next to a pump, as if filling up. She passes by.

Thirteen miles further down the road, Augusta stops at one of the highway's rest-stops.

Evan positions the larger SNAG onto a branch of the only tree nearby. It's parched and leafless.

We ride past her, turning down a road not far from it.

From there, we see Augusta get out of her truck and go to the middle concrete table on the row farthest from the highway. She sits dead center on one of its concrete benches. After placing her hands under the table, she leans forward. Finally she finds what she's looking for:

A black rectangle, no bigger than a shoe box.

Augusta gets into her truck and drives away.

Evan summons the raven SNAG to follow overhead.

The flying beetle SNAG picks up her verbal command to her truck's GPS: "Horseshoe Creek Mine."

I do the same to ours. "That circles us back down Highway 85, somewhere in the hills just beyond the road where she'll turn off for her ranch," I tell Jack.

"Emma, any idea what this location is, exactly?" Jack asks.

"Give me a moment," she says. Then: "It's an abandoned mineshaft. It was opened in the mid-19th Century after someone struck gold for all of five minutes. Let me see if I can pull up its geological survey." A minute later she lets loose with a long, low whistle. "The shaft burrows down below their property and ends just a few feet from the launch command and control facility."

"Is she planting an explosive device?" I ask.

"Not if Russia is keeping to its playbook. More than likely the device's placement will allow Russia to track signal transmissions being sent to and from the facility, including any launch commands," Jack replies.

"Evan, so that we can trace the device's location, make sure one of the small SNAGs goes into the shaft with Augusta," I suggest.

"Great idea," Evan replies. "Then, when she clears out, I'll go in and hack the device."

"She's now a mile and a half ahead of me," Abu lets us know. "I'll stop a quarter of a mile beyond her turn-off so that she won't see me."

"We're on our way," Jack tells him.

"By the way, Yelena is just an hour away from the Cheyenne airport," Emma says. "Her pilot hasn't yet submitted his flight plan to Air Traffic Control."

"Unless he's also SVR, I'll bet she keeps it to herself until she's ready to be wheels up," I reply.

Jack frowns. "If not, hopefully, he'll survive this grand tour of hers. But I wouldn't bet on it."

WHEN WE REACH THE TURNOFF TO THE MINE, WE PARK A quarter of a mile beyond it.

The raven SNAG allows us to see that Augusta has reached the mine. It's a good thing her truck has four-wheel drive because a recent storm has turned the road into nothing more than two deep ruts almost wheel high.

When Augusta gets out of her truck, she's carrying the device Yelena left for her.

The mine doesn't have much of a door: just a few ancient planks hinged together. A small boulder—solid and weighty—has been propped against it to keep it closed.

Holding onto the black box, Augusta nudges the rock out of the way with her boot. Her grunts reflect the severity of the task. When she's done, she tucks the box under one arm before grabbing hold of the door's rusted hook and lifting it before elbowing the door open. She pulls out a small flashlight that was hooked to her belt.

Evan has perched the raven SNAG on a cliff on the hill

across from the mine. He waits until she's inside before sending the beetle SNAG in after her. It takes a few moments for its night-vision adjustment to kick in.

The mine is a catacomb of rooms. She seems to be using a map to find her way. It takes her all the way through to the back of the mine. She climbs onto an outcropping and nudges the box high onto a beam on the back wall, then flips a switch.

As she turns to leave, she's distracted by something:

Darn it—she hears the beetle SNAG's faint buzzing and is looking around for it.

"Evan, move it away from her," I hiss.

He maneuvers it up. As it backs off, we hear screeches and loud scuffling.

Augusta squeals, "Oh, goodness!"

"Ah, just great!" Jack mutters. "There's a handful of bats in the cave, and they're after the SNAG! Get it out of there, Evan."

"On it!" Evan's fingers move furiously on the joystick. At the same time, Augusta screams, "Oh, my lord, my lord!..." as she swats at the bats. Suddenly she yells, "Ouch! Darn!"

"She's been bit!" Abu says.

As Augusta falls to her knees, her map drops into a muddy puddle.

"Darn it!" Augusta fumbles for the paper. It's smeared with mud—unreadable—and so damp that it disintegrates in her hand. Cursing, she stumbles to her feet and lurches out.

In no time she's lost.

"Hello!... *Hello?* I'm a U.S. Park ranger. Is anyone there?" It's Abu.

"Please, keep talking! I'm lost and I need to hear your voice!" Augusta is teary and breathless.

"No problem. I have a flashlight. You can also follow my light." Abu starts singing *Staying Alive.*

Who knew he had a decent falsetto? Gee, the dude has so many hidden talents.

In time she finds him. Flinging herself into his arms, she exclaims, "I had a map, but I lost my way!"

He coughs as he pats her back. I'm assuming he's trying to cover up the beetle SNAG's faint buzz as Evan maneuvers it out of the mine shaft.

"I know amateur prospectors go in and out of these places, but because of its instability, we'll soon be closing up this particular mine. Its rafters are rotten. You'll probably be the last person to walk through it."

Augusta's relief flattens into a frown. "Maybe it's for the best," she mutters. When she pulls back from him, she can no longer look him in the eye. "Thank you again. Now, if you'll excuse me."

"Sure, no problem." Abu's tone is cheery.

She can't get into her truck fast enough. He waves as she drives off.

We wait for her to turn back onto Highway 85 and toward the direction of her ranch. We then turn onto the mine's road ourselves. By the time we reach the shaft, Abu has grabbed the SNAGs. He walks into the mine with Evan, securing lamps on a few of the mine's high beams all the way to where Augusta left the device.

Too disturbed by our activity and the lights, the bats flee. I shiver as they fly into the tallest tree beside the mine's entrance.

Jack puts his arm around me.

I sigh. "I wonder if we'll ever know why Augusta did it."

He shrugs. "As long as we can beat the Russians with our disinformation, she'll get away with it. For her, it's better than the alternative."

"You mean, spending the rest of her life in prison for treason?"

"Or getting a bullet to the head from Yelena, who knows she's a loose end."

"You're right. Augusta can identify her," I acknowledge.

"We're heading back to the plane," Jack tells Abu and Evan. "Meet you there."

We're about a half-mile from the Nickerson ranch when two ambulances pass us, and a firetruck.

We watch as they turn into the Nickersons' driveway.

Jack stops the car.

"Emma, what just happened at the Nickerson ranch?" I ask.

"Let me see what police chatter I can pick up," she suggests.

A moment later Emma responds: "They're calling it a murder-suicide. It looks as if Frank shot her, and then himself."

"Wait… So, did he know what she did? Is that why he shot her?"

"I...I don't know. But I suspect..." I hear Emma tapping her keyboard.

The next thing I see on my cell is an aerial view of the ranch.

"Look at the time stamp," Emma says."

"Looks like it indicates forty minutes ago." Jack and I watch as a car pulls out of the road from the Nickersons' home. Like us, it's going south on 85.

"I'll bet this rental car will be at Cheyenne Regional when you fly out," Emma says.

Of course it will. It was used by Yelena.

Jack is right: there will be no loose ends.

12

Act Your Age!

CONSIDERING ALL THAT IT TAKES TO BE A CONSUMMATE HOSTESS —stamina, grace under pressure, diplomacy, and the ability to delegate—is it no wonder that the best ones also demonstrate a modicum of maturity, no matter your actual age?

(Hint: No one suggests you bandy about that vicious number. In fact, such candor is greatly discouraged…)

Here's how to demonstrate a wise demeanor no matter those incidents that might make you throw a tantrum that would make a toddler proud:

First, take a deep breath. Count to ten. Or twenty. Or even fifty. In other words, do whatever you can to keep from exploding in anger at whoever is making you blow your stack. (Unless they've broken something extremely valuable. At that point, their disappearance from your presence should be swift. And painful. And permanent if it was a family heirloom.)

Next, time for some visualization techniques. No matter

who has made you angry, envision them naked. This gives you complete control over your emotions.

(However, to have complete control over the perpetrators, you must do something entirely different, like, strip them of their clothes and let their departure be the walk of shame they deserve.)

Finally, if someone insults you, smile and pretend you didn't hear them. *(Unless the insult has something to do with your age. At that point, being accused of being hard of hearing is the last thing you need. Instead, to prove you've still got a steady hand, pistol practice is in order. Even if the bullet ends up in your insulter, you've proven your point:*

That they should never mess with you!)

BY THE TIME WE BOARD THE PLANE AGAIN, ARNIE IS ALREADY on it.

"When we're in flight, Ryan wants to talk to us," he explains.

At twenty thousand feet, we turn on the monitor. Ryan's face fills it. "Yelena's pilot finally filed his flight plan," he informs us. "You're headed to Bossier City, Louisiana."

"What joys does that little burgh hold for us?" I ask.

"It's adjacent to Barksdale AFB, which is not only home to the 2nd Bomb Squad's three squadrons of 42H Stratofortress bombers but also the Air Force Global Strike Command. We assume this last entity is Yelena's target."

"Why is that?" Jack asks.

"Recently, Barksdale became the first of two AFGSC bases to receive and implement the latest and greatest nuclear command, control, and communications system—or NC3," Ryan explains. "Essentially, it's a 'command-post-in-a-box.' The system is modular, and its speed allows for greater lethality. It will survive chemical, nuclear, radiological, biological, and high-yield explosive attacks, not to mention high-altitude electromagnetic pulse environments. Barksdale is the first installation before it's rolled out on the other bases."

Ryan and Emma's faces are replaced with the photo of a young Air Force captain in uniform; twentyish, buff, blondish.

"Ten minutes ago, Yelena texted a burner phone. We traced its coordinates to the on-base housing duplex of Captain Kyle Bender, a cyber warfare engineer," Emma explains. "They're to meet at the Spring Creek Suites, just outside the base, in Bossier City. She's handing him a thumb drive that will release a virus that mirrors the new system's coding and commands back to Russia. In return for him uploading it into the NC3 system, she'll also hand over the password to the Swiss bank account where they've parked his payoff."

Ryan adds: "After we've blocked any calls coming in or going out from his burner, 'she'—that is, Donna—will text him at the same number, moving the meeting up by an hour. Then 'Kyle'—again, an Acme operative—will meet with the real Yelena to take the one Russia wants him to have so that we can analyze the intel they're seeking and send misinformation instead."

Jack clears his throat. "So, I guess that means we're following the same protocol as on the Jim Creek mission." He gives me a sidelong glance.

"Yes," Ryan declares. "Only Evan, not you, will be doubling as Kyle. He's closest to his age and his build."

Thank goodness!...

Oh…

Heck.

Evan turns red. Noting the rest of the team's stares, he turns away.

"And Donna will honeypot the actual Kyle." Ryan scrutinizes us. "I assume we're all fine with this?"

"Yes, sir," I say.

Evan's acknowledgement comes out as a croak, but I guess he's just given his tacit approval.

"Yelena has reserved a room on the ground floor," Ryan continues. "Arnie, you and Abu will be given the room to her left. It's the closest to her television. You can hack its cable feed and use the monitor as Acme's in-room camera. Jack will take the room on the right, which also shares an adjoining door. The same thing regarding Donna's rooms, which are on the other side of the building. Emma will have eyes and ears on everyone from this side. You'll need to create Donna and Evan's new faces before your land, so get on it."

He's gone.

A good thing, too, because Evan goes into the sleeping cabin and slams the door.

Jack shrugs. "I'll give him a few minutes and then talk to him."

"What will you say?" I ask.

"That I know exactly how he feels. Should he decide to do it, he's not being disloyal to the one he loves." He shakes his head. "I'll also explain that…that she'll understand."

"How do you know?" I argue. "It isn't easy for either of us and it won't be for Evan, either. Or for Mary. The reality is this: it's a mission. What happens is classified intel. We don't talk about what goes on. He needs to know that."

"He does, Donna!" Jack's annoyance is clear. "Still, if you love someone, you never want to hurt them."

"As if I don't know that!" Does he hear the tremble in my voice?

Jack puts his arm around me. "I get it. The ball is in his court. And as we both know all too well, following through on the mission never leaves you with a clean conscience. You still know you've let down your partner. And… Mary will know it too."

"If he tells her," I murmur.

Jack smirks. "They've been testing the strength of their love since they met. Do you think he won't come clean about it?"

"What will you advise him to do?"

Jack sighs. "If he asks, I'd say the truth. As we both know, it comes out one way or another."

Poor Evan.

Poor Mary.

AN HOUR LATER, EVAN TEXTS JACK. AFTER READING THE missive, he nods. "Off to the races. Wish me luck."

Ha, luck!

Admittedly, we've caught a few breaks by the skin of our chinny chin chins. But so much can—and will—go wrong.

A half-hour later, Jack and Evan join the rest of us. While Arnie plays a video game, Abu puts the finishing touches on my face—that is, Yelena's.

Evan's forced smile disappears altogether when he sees me. Looking away, he says, "I've agreed to do what's necessary."

"We know you will," I assure him.

Without looking up, Arnie says, "Hey, you can always tell her you've got the clap."

No one laughs.

At least, not until Evan does.

KYLE'S KNOCK ON THE DOOR TO MY HOME CREEK SUITES room is too cocky by half: *Shave and a Haircut—Two Bits.*

When I open it, his wolf whistle is just as annoying. "*Yes, ma'am!* You are *much better* than I pictured you."

"No need to tell the whole world. Shut up and get in here." I take a step back.

He takes a step forward so that he's chest to breast with me.

When I push back, he slaps me down. I don't have time

to reach for the Acme Love potion. Instinctively. I scramble onto the bed—

Which is precisely where he wants me. He knees me in the back, pinning me onto the bed. My sundress is now over my head. He twists my thong so tightly that I'm relieved when it finally rips. "Yahoo! *Trophy*—one of many I'll be taking from you today, my little Russian doll. So tell me: there's gotta be a cherry you haven't popped, right?" To make his point, he slaps my ass. "Hey? Have you tried asphyxiation yet?... NO? *Alright, alright, alright!* That means I'll be your first! I'm hard just knowing that!" He then leans over me and whispers in my ear: "Seeing how you Russian sparrows have been trained by the best, what say you give me an around-the-world tour? Show me all the tricks of the trade. We'll save the choke-and-poke for the finale." The next thing I know, his hand is between my legs, grappling too roughly, too deeply. "Don't you worry none, girly. This is one deal you'll get your money's worth."

My money's worth.

Right now, my husband and the young man I've raised as a son are watching this. I can only imagine their shock; their fierce desire to come to my rescue.

Nothing is worth this:

Not the infliction of pain on my body. Not the degradation that seers deep into my soul.

My hand shoots out for something, anything that will make that point. I find it: a pen on the bedside table.

With a flick of a Bic, he's now a stuck prick—in a

manner of speaking. Frankly, he's lucky I didn't stick him *there.*

Then again, had I done so as opposed to his jugular vein, he wouldn't be convulsing through his death rattle.

Oh, bother. Because he's collapsed on top of me. I'm now covered in his blood.

This dress is trashed.

So is this mission.

Ah, hell. Ryan will be livid.

JACK BURSTS THROUGH THE DOOR. "JESUS, DONNA!... WHEN I realized what he was doing, I got here as quickly as I...." Jack takes notes of my unbecoming predicament. Then, shaking his head: "I'd hope to stop him from doing *that* so you wouldn't have to do *this.*"

"So sorry, dear. As fast as he was moving, I thought it better not to wait for the Cavalry to arrive." I point to Kyle, who's still convulsing as he drains blood. "A little help please?"

As Jack flings the serviceman's body to one side, I sit up, tucking the skirt of my blood-soaked dress down around my thighs. "I'm sorry I gave the boys such a show, especially Evan," I mutter.

Speaking of the devil, Evan bursts through the adjoining door even as Abu tries to hold him back.

I'm shaking as I get to my feet. "I'm okay, Evan. Truly, I am. Just...embarrassed."

Three steps later, he's at my side. He hugs me tightly. "Donna…I'm…I'm so sorry."

I tweak his nose—that is, Kyle's. "You have nothing to apologize for. Sadly, this happens more often than I'd care to admit…."

Especially now, considering the look of disgust on his face.

I know it's not at me when he declares, "I'm glad Mary made the decision to choose a different profession."

I pull back from him. "Good to know. Wish I'd had the same choice, but sometimes real life presents circumstances that forces a change in course."

Evan's face falls. "I…I didn't mean that the way it sounded!"

"Don't worry. You didn't insult me." How could he? His eyes are wide open to who I am and what I do.

What I *must* do to accomplish my missions.

To stay alive.

I'm strong enough to let it roll off my back. Wish I could have done the same with Kyle. Instead, Arnie is loading him into a laundry cart and wheeling him into the adjacent room.

It dawns on me: "We've got a real problem on our hands now: who will embed the trojan on Barksdale's console?"

"Strip Kyle down to his skivvies," Jack tells him. "Evan will need his uniform to go onto the base and put the trojan in place."

Evan's eyes grow large. "Me?"

Jack nods. "Who else? You heard Ryan. You're going to be Kyle to complete your mission."

"But…"

"No buts," Jack growls.

I take hold of Evan's arm. "What's wrong? Are you worried that you won't be able to convince Yelena?"

Evan's eyes narrow. "No. Not anymore. Not after what happened to you."

Me?

He thinks he's avenging me…

Maybe I'm not the issue. Perhaps it has more to do with his ability to live with himself.

Evan has a very long road ahead of him: one in which snap decisions can and will change his life.

Gently, I kiss his cheek. "Go with your gut. No regrets."

As he walks away, Jack mutters, "Easier said than done."

We leave Evan and Arnie to analyze the algorithm and plant the trojan.

AN HOUR LATER, EVAN KNOCKS ON YELENA'S DOOR.

When she opens it, through Evan's Acme lenses, we see she's wearing a white terry bathrobe. It's not tied. As Evan's eyes scan her, we also see that what little there is of her Brazilian suggests she's a blonde.

Evan shoves her out of the way. "Show me the money," he snarls.

She lifts a burner phone from the room's desk. "Shall I make the transfer?"

"I'll do it. What's the passcode?"

She tells him.

As he punches it in, he tells her: "Bow on the bed with your back to me. Wait for me there."

Silently she does as she's told. Her sly smile seems to anticipate his demand for submission. Though she had yet to meet him, she read him like a book.

It's why he was easy to turn.

Immediately, Evan transfers half a million dollars into another offshore account controlled by Acme. He puts the cell in his pocket. The tips of his fingers have a scrim that keeps their prints off all surfaces. Here's hoping we'll finally have Yelena's. As a failsafe, Arnie and Abu will also dust the room for prints. She's got to show up in some database somewhere: ours or an ally's.

In assuming the commanded position, Yelena has also disrobed. Evan now strips the robe of its sash. With it, he ties her wrists to the bedpost and then yanks her legs, so they are stretched out behind her.

He then goes into the bathroom. When he comes back, he's got a washcloth with him. He stuffs it into Yelena's mouth.

She isn't anticipating this. Her eyes go wide—

But not for long. He takes a case off one of the pillows and puts it over her head. Her mutterings are gagged.

Evan then unbuckles his belt and pulls it free of his pants.

The beating is harsh and slow, lashing her back. She grunts but stays in position.

We can't see her eyes but her fingers clench as she feels each lash.

When Evan is done with her, she's heaving from the pain. He leans in and whispers: "Now I've got my money's worth."

He said it with Kyle's hard-edged drawl. In fact, in every sense, Evan embodies the airman.

No, to be honest, his acts of cruelty were his own.

After he leaves, she stays on the bed. In time, she inches up until she's crouching. By twisting her wrists, she loosens one arm and then the other.

It takes her a while to get off the bed. She's in too much pain. When she does, she limps to the bathroom and starts a bath.

While it fills with water, she makes her way to the desk and pulls out her cell phone from a drawer. She walks back into the bathroom but doesn't shut the door.

"Emma, can you pick up audio via the monitor feed?" Jack asks.

"Barely, but yeah. Yelena is speaking in Russian… Something about what a bastard Kyle is, and that she wants it assured that he will meet with an accident some-time next year."

"She'll learn soon enough that her wish was granted," I reply.

Evan confirms that he's headed over to the base. With Kyle's credentials, he'll slip in, do what he has to do, and slip back out.

By the time he returns, he'll have processed the anger he took out on Yelena.

At least, I hope so.

One thing's for sure: I don't think he should be asked to play such a role again.

13

Cosplay Party!

W ANT TO SHAKE UP YOUR SOIRÉE? CONSIDER A COSPLAY *(costume play) theme! Here are some recommended rules:*

1: Make it something with lots of different characters so there's a less likely chance that everyone will look alike.

How un-fun is it when every woman in the joint shows up as a cinnamon bun-eared Princess Leia, either in a leather bikini or white robe? The guys may like this, but the ladies are left flirting with Obiwans (ancients), Darth Vaders (sadistic arseholes), and Yodas (undatable for the simple reason that they have faces only a mother could love). Let's face it: the chance of Han Solo sweeping you off your feet is slim to none.

2: Invite those who you really want to be there.

Again, use this Star Wars scene as the ultimate anti-example. Even if the goal is to fill the room, the last thing you need is to find yourself in a live version of Oga's Cantina: that smoky, dimly lit tavern in Tatooine filled with undesirables who chug strong drinks before intermittently breaking out into fights.

3: Condemn any hazardous props.

Sticking with the tried-and-true Star Wars *scenario: Everybody and his brother will bring a lightsaber. But when your house catches fire because some idiot brought the real thing, you'll wish you'd chosen a safer theme like* Squid Game. *Seriously: what could possibly go wrong?*

"As we suspected, Yelena's flight plan indicates that her next stop is in fact Offutt AFB," Emma informs us. "It's right outside of Omaha."

"Then, Ryan's assumption is correct: the base is an important target for Yelena because of the missiles under its command," Jack reasons.

"Yes," Emma confirms. "It's the host station to the 55th Wing, the largest of the USAF's Air Combat Commands. It's also the headquarters of USSTRATCOM—that is, the US Strategic Command Headquarters. But, oddly, Yelena has yet to contact her operative there. Usually, she does so the moment she's reached cruising altitude."

"She's sure to send off a communique sometime during the flight," I suggest. "I guess all we can do is sit tight and wait."

"Agreed. I'll call back as soon as I know more," Emma promises.

Though the flight is only two and a half hours, Abu,

Arnie, and Jack have nodded off. However, Evan is awake. He pretends he's reading, but it's been five minutes since he turned a page in his book. He just stares at it.

Plopping down in the captain's chair beside his, I ask, "A penny for your thoughts?"

He doesn't turn to me. His voice is low. Still, I make out his words: "I didn't know I had it in me."

"Are you talking about what you did with…to Yelena?"

He nods. "I've never been so angry—so filled with hate." He hangs his head. "Donna, I… *I could have killed her.*"

"Why do you think that is?"

"Because I hate what she's doing to our country! In that regard, she reminds me of… of my mother." Evan shrugs. "I guess it's the ultimate Oedipal complex."

The woman who bore him, Catherine McMartin, was to be president of the United States—a position that would have put our country in a grave situation:

Catherine was a Quorum operative.

Her husband, Robert—my first crush and once a dear friend—found out about it and was going to let the world know.

She had him murdered.

Carl carried out the assassination.

Evan whispers, "I should have killed Yelena."

"If you'd done that, our mission would have failed. All we'd done up to that point would have been for naught."

"It's why I walked away," he admits.

I pat his arm. "You did the right thing. I can say that because sometimes I've felt exactly the same way."

His eyes seek out mine. "Donna, I vow on my father's grave: I will never harm Mary."

"I know that, Evan. In fact, now more than ever, I know how far you'd go to protect her."

He nods, then takes a deep breath. "About Mary: should I... you know, explain?"

What can I tell him about that oftentimes niggling reality we call the truth?

That sometimes it hurts?

That we're tempted to shoot the messenger?

That some acts are unforgivable?

Are others just as odious but necessary to make the world better?

Evan wants to hear from me that Mary will understand why he made the choice he did and that she will accept it as the best-case scenario.

"I really don't know how Mary will react." There, I've said it.

He'll soon find out.

Had Evan been a different person—one who hadn't seen the evil of treason up close—perhaps he would have done the same as most other men:

Fucked her and left it at that.

Like Jack has told me repeatedly, emotions have nothing to do with it.

So why do I still find it so hard to believe?

Poor Mary.

"Wake up, sleeping beauties." Our pilot, George, shakes my shoulder and Evan's simultaneously.

The best I can do is open one eye. Evan practically leaps up. To make himself wake up, he shakes his head.

"Big Poom-bah needs everyone's attention." He leans in to tap the monitor.

Jack, Arnie, and Abu are already rubbing the sleep from their eyes. I guess I should force mine open too.

"Whatever Yelena has planned for Offutt, we can assume the worst: that it's going to be big, and it's going to be bad." Ryan isn't wasting any time.

"Well, hello to you too," I murmur.

Ryan barks, "What did you say, Mrs. Craig?"

I fake a cough. "Nothing, sir! Something was caught in my throat."

His grunt indicates he's only warily accepting my answer. But putting me in my place takes a backseat to the bigger fish Ryan's got to fry: "As I was saying, while we don't know exactly what Yelena has planned, it's been announced that President Kentfield will be touring the base, which complicates our mission considerably. Also on this boondoggle are Energy Secretary Robert Walden and the head of the National Nuclear Security Administration, Doris Riordan. I'm sure the Kremlin has made Yelena aware of the situation. If so, her mission may now be POTUS's assassination—perhaps via the total annihilation of the region."

"Can Marcus gently suggest to POTUS that she postpone the trip?" Jack suggests.

"Too late. They'll be landing just an hour after you're in Omaha. Besides, President Kentfield would ask why. But knowing there is a mole somewhere in the Administration, it's best to keep her on a need-to-know basis. Instead, we'll have you shadowing POTUS in plain sight."

"How?" Abu asks.

"As part of the journalists' pool," Emma replies. "The whole mission team still has its Hart Media press credentials. Jack will again resume the moniker 'Grant Larkin' while Donna will again be the British reporter, 'Gwendolyn Durant.' Abu and Arnie will go as camera crew, and Evan as a photographer."

"What happens if we spot Yelena?" I ask.

"If between now and the event we learn that her mission is to be a lethal threat to POTUS, we'll pass this intel forward to Marcus so that the Secret Service can do what it does best: protect and defend. However, if for some reason POTUS's detail is out of reach, do what's necessary to make sure Yelena fails," Ryan explains. "Until then, we should go under the assumption that our target is there to initiate a brush pass. In other words, keep to the protocol: watch for it, intercept it, analyze the intel, and alter it as necessary without raising Yelena's suspicions." He lets that sink in. "You'll be landing soon, so work on your covers. Good luck, team."

ONCE AGAIN, BY DONNING A SHORTISH ASH BLONDE WIG, BLUE lenses, and a prosthetic that gives my nose a slight bump, I'm transformed into Hart Media's international correspondent, Gwendolyn Durant, known for her piercing questions relayed in a dulcet-toned stiff-upper-lip British accent.

For Jack's transition, Abu shortens and lightens my husband's hair. Jack also wears a pair of sturdy glasses and has traded his jeans and AIR FORCE tee-shirt for a custom Brioni suit and smart John Lobb Becketts.

Our press credentials get us into a conga line of journalists jostling for a prime photo-op position. The tour begins on the tarmac with a Q&A with the squadron leader of the Fighting Fifty-Fifth. It's followed by an airshow.

By the final flyover, President Kentfield and her entourage have also arrived on the tarmac. While the statesman slaps each pilot on their back, POTUS returns their salutes before shaking each one's hand.

We're then hustled into a small auditorium. The journalists take their seats in the front row while the photographers kneel in front of the raised stage. Videographers work the sides of the stage. The rest of the seats are filled with service personnel.

The presentation starts with a video highlighting the latest and greatest technological advances of the crowning component of our national security: its nuclear missiles program. Showcased are the underground bunkers and the personnel who oversee them twenty-four seven. The journalists oooh and ahhh from vertigo when the camera rides shotgun with the pilots who crisscross baby blue skies in state-of-the-art aircraft.

When the lights go on, Energy Secretary Walden is at the podium. Others are now seated in the row of chairs behind him. National Nuclear Security Administrator Riordan and Marcus Branham are also onstage—

As is Senator Bennington and his wife, Crystal—

Who has Mary by her side.

Mario stands to one side of the stage, scanning the room.

Our eyes meet. He smirks, then taps his nose to acknowledge the change in mine.

Why, that son of a bitch! I'd guessed right: this is his way of putting Mary in the crossroads of this mission.

As an aide to the congressperson who heads the committee in charge of nuclear intelligence—or in this case, an aide to his wife—she can report any suspicious actions to Mario.

All this time, I've been wondering where Yelena is hiding. Now I see her:

Auburn-haired and wearing glasses, she is on the other side of Senator Bennington and whispering something into his ear. Whatever it is, he likes what he's hearing.

Crystal Bennington also notices the interchange. She frowns, obviously annoyed, as is Mary.

Does Mario already know that Yelena is the mole?

Does Bennington know?

Or is he a willing asset?

I say willing because of the familiar way Yelena touches

his shoulder: allowing it to linger, as does her smile when his eyes caress her.

And yes, Crystal sees this too.

Noting her distress, Mary hands Crystal a note that earns her a nod and a forced smile.

"—With no further ado, I'd like to hand the microphone over to our Commander in Chief, Libby Kentfield," Energy Secretary Walden announces.

A roar of applause meets POTUS as she enters the room from offstage. She waves gleefully at the crowd, then launches into an inspirational speech about hard work, dedication, our country's military superiority, and the vigilance we must always keep foremost in our minds if we're to defeat the enemies that live for the downfall of our country.

"As much as I'd like to take credit for the idea of Global Strike Command, I can't," she continues. "And while every person in this room has brought the idea to fruition and will assure its safety, viability, and success so that the rest of us can sleep at night, it was the brainchild of a visionary who knew our adversaries well enough to live by this Theodore Roosevelt quote: 'Speak softly and carry a big stick.' I wish to call on him to share the accolades that truly belong to him: former president Lee Chiffray."

Lee…

Is here?

But of course he is. Lee's background is in technology. And he's always been a visionary.

Not to mention he's seen evil up close.

I sit up as he walks to the podium. When he scans the room, our eyes meet.

He gawks. He'd been interviewed by "Gwendolyn" before, up close and personal. Even then, he knew me so well that this disguise didn't fool him.

Our eyes break away when he realizes the deafening applause is his cue to go onstage and take questions from the press.

I certainly have a few for him.

As he makes his way to the stage, Evan sees Mary. Flustered, Evan drops his camera. Thank goodness it's strapped to his neck. He fumbles to hold it up to his face again but it's too late:

Mary has noticed him. Her jaw drops. Her cheeks are now as red as his.

Oh, dear.

Her eyes scan the rest of the press corps. I see her eyes widen when she recognizes Abu. She rolls her eyes when she sees Arnie.

I feel a tap on my shoulder: Mario squats beside me and whispers in my ear: "Fancy meeting you here."

"A heads-up would have been nice," I retort. I nod toward Mary. "If she doesn't keep her cool, she'll blow our mission sky high."

"Don't you worry about her," he assures me. "She's working out like a dream." Mario cranes his neck. "So that I don't blow your cover, what say we play catch-up later?"

With that, he slips away, entering the stage from the back. He kneels next to Mary and whispers something in her ear.

Hopefully, he's not stupid enough to tell her that I'm here—

Oops, too late for that. Following Mario's nod, she now sees me too.

A wig and the crook in my nose are not exactly an invisibility shield to someone who grew up studying my inflections, profile, and body language.

But before she looks away, she gives me a wink.

That's my girl.

THE QUESTIONS FROM THE PRESS COME FAST AND FURIOUSLY. Libby and Lee take turns volleying them. Eventually, they call Chad Bennington onto the stage so that he can share the spotlight.

I jump up when the base's press officer warns us that there is only time for one more question.

"Mr. Chiffray, how very jolly to see you back in your element, especially while enjoying the fruition of this exemplary program that was your brainchild. I remember you mentioning it in passing when we'd last met. I also remember you'd promised me an exclusive interview. Perhaps you have time for it today?" Despite my deferential tone, Lee knows me too well:

It's no idle request for chitchat.

"But of course. Now, in fact, Ms...." His helpless shrug is accompanied by a sly grin. "I'm sorry, I've forgotten your name."

"Gwendolyn Durant. Hart Media."

"By all means, Ms. Durant." He motions the base's press secretary to the side. After a few words, she nods for me to follow her.

When I reach them, she says, "You can use my office. When you're done, my assistant will escort you out."

I follow her.

Lee is a few steps behind, as is his Secret Service detail, Porter included.

I feel the eyes of others on us: When I turn around, I see that Jack doesn't look too pleased.

For that matter, neither does Yelena.

The press secretary leads us down a long corridor to an office, then closes the door behind her.

And just in the nick of time. Lee's snickering has him doubled over.

"KEEP IT DOWN," I SCOLD HIM.

This only makes Lee chortle gleefully. "If it's any consolation, I'm not laughing at you, despite my surprise in catching you playing Lois Lane, star reporter, yet again." He takes my fake glasses and wipes off a smudge with his kerchief before handing them back. "Jack was practically bristling at you for wrangling some alone time with me."

"He was bristling at you, not me," I huff. "And the thought that I was wrangling for some alone time is wishful thinking on your part."

"Once again, you dash my hopes with your cruelty, Mrs. Craig."

"Lee, I'm dead serious! Outside that door is a Russian agent crisscrossing the country, sabotaging our military bases."

When what I say registers, all joy leaves his face. "Have you identified him?"

"We have indeed," I assure him, "only it's a her. Senator Bennington's aide, in fact."

Slowly, Lee sits down. "Lara Owensby?... But... That's impossible! She's been with Chad for years! Well, at least all the time I've known him. Four...maybe five years now."

"By the way, her real name is Yelena, albeit that's more than likely an alias too. And considering that Bennington chairs the Senate Subcommittee on Strategic Forces, she's well placed for knowing who, what, and where to build her counterintelligence network, wouldn't you say?"

Speechless, he can only nod.

"Chad's wife, Crystal, doesn't seem too enthralled with her," I point out.

Lee shrugs. "Why would she be? He chases anything in a skirt."

"Including Lara—that is, Yelena," I point out.

"Quite frankly, no. Lara made it pretty clear to him that she's in a relationship."

"I guess that's what she told him to take time off last week: to be with her quote-unquote boyfriend."

Lee sighs. "As a matter of fact, she claimed she was with an ill parent. But three weeks ago, she spent time with the guy she's been seeing."

"How do you know?"

"Because…" Lee hesitates, then looks away. "Because… I'm him."

"Oh!…"

Shite.

This isn't Lee's first rodeo with spies as lovers. His now-deceased wife, Babette, was an operative with the Quorum.

I stay silent. No need to rub it in since the same terrorist organization also turned my first and now very dead husband, Carl.

Sheesh! We sure know how to pick'em.

14

Surprise Guests

As far as a hostess is concerned, there's a special circle of hell for those who show up to a party without being invited!

Should she ignore the fact and let them attend anyway? Just as horrifically, should she allow guests who didn't RSVP?

Um—NO.

There are ways to let interlopers know they've crossed a line. These include:

1: Tell them you've reached the occupancy threshold that the fire department says is safe. Then close the door with a sad face because you pull it off so well.

2: Put them in a waiting area. Preferably in the cellar, where your invited partygoers can't hear them. Lock the door. By the third day, they'll get the message: don't mess with me.

3: When all else fails, slam the door in their faces. Will they be miffed? Most definitely. Will you care? Not one iota. Should you be worried that such truculent behavior may do

*irreparable damage to your reputation? Not at all! If anything,
you'll be legendary!*

Especially if, at first, you've greeted them with a shotgun.

*Your true friends will insist that "a cooler head prevailed—
allowing them to keep theirs."*

They know of what they speak.

I TELL LEE EVERYTHING.

I do this because he has to carry on in front of her as if
he doesn't know *anything*.

As if he's still smitten with her.

As if being with her makes him feel he hasn't a care in
the world.

And now, knowing who she is means he'll also know
what not to say to her, even if she asks all the wrong questions in a seemingly innocent fashion.

I tell Lee everything because I trust him with my life.

It won't be the first time.

When I'm through with my briefing, he bows his head
and groans.

"How long have you been dating?" I ask.

And why didn't I know about it before now?

Yes, I want to ask this. I can't help it.

"About a month. I attended the United Nations'
Conference on Disarmament. Libby was there, and so was
Lara and the Senator."

"Lee, I need to know…."

Oh, dear.

Well, here goes: "Have you been intimate with her?"

"I can't tell you the number of times I'd wished you'd have asked me that very question—out of jealousy, of course!" His chuckle is raucous. "But, nah. Instead, it's because I'm suddenly a national security risk." He paces the room. "Okay yeah: we've fucked. She's a dream in that department. Too good, in fact. That should have been the tip-off. The tricks of the trade, right? Babette was like that too. At first, anyway."

Until she had what she wanted from him: money and power.

Until Babette fell in love with Salem Rahmin al-Sadah, whose wealth was legion. One of his pet projects was funding the Quorum.

Another was screwing Babette when she was the First Lady.

Lee's anxiety has him raking his fingers through his hair. "Tell me what I should do. Should I suddenly be too busy? Drop her cold turkey?"

"No," I insist. She can't suspect anyone knows, so, um…keep it business as usual."

Lee grimaces. "That's not the metaphor I'd have used before this conversation, but it works now."

"Also, Lee: it's important that you—and Acme—have eyes and ears on her at all times in case she does something that might compromise you too. Is she going back to Washington with the senator?"

He guffaws. "No. In fact, the Kentfields and the Benningtons are my guests for the next two days at my ranch, the Triple L. We'll be playing golf, going horseback riding, fishing—"

"Your ranch is near here?"

"Just a few miles away, across the Iowa state line. In fact, they flew directly there. I have my own landing strip."

"Of course you do," I say dryly. "My bad. I never asked where your ranch was. I just assumed it was in Nevada or Texas." Then I remember: "Aunt Phyllis and the kids are also there!"

Lee frowns. "Do you think they're in danger?"

"Considering Yelena is within spitting distance of the current president and spit-swappingly cozy with a former POTUS, I'd say yeah." Now I'm the one pacing the room. "Ryan must be freaking out. We're to safeguard Libby at all costs."

"I imagine we have the bases covered between her Secret Service detail and mine."

"Here's the thing, Lee: This mission was to uncover a mole in the administration. Because Yelena is on Bennington's staff, we can't out her just yet. We've spent the past week shadowing her all over the country, counter-sabotaging her efforts to undermine our missile defense system. This was the last stop on her magical mystery tour. If my team does its job right, we must stop whatever she's got planned for you and your guests but still allow her to think she got away with her other bad deeds."

He snaps his fingers. "In that case, you've got the perfect cover. I'm inviting you and your camera crew to do that exclusive interview I supposedly promised you. Spend as long as you need with us."

"Jack and I will just have to stay away from our kids so that they don't blow our cover."

"No problem. I'll send them off on a camping trip for the next few days."

"Perfect! Our next dilemma is putting eyes and ears on Yelena at all times. But I assume Triple L Ranch isn't a sixty-room castle like Lion's Lair."

Lee groans. "Bigger. More like seventy. In fact, Triple L stands for 'Larger Lion's Lair.'"

"And all this time, I thought it was a rough-hewn hacienda with a few heads of cattle that fed some weird fantasy you have to play cowboy."

"Well, I fooled you. It's a real working ranch—and so successful that I can no longer use it as a write-off. I've got five hundred head of prime Grade-A Angus roaming seven hundred thousand acres," he admits. "As for tracking Lara—that is, Yelena—you're free to hack Triple L's security feed."

"Thanks. Also…" Oh dear, how do I put this delicately? "Lee, she has probably already assessed your security procedures and is aware of any rooms that aren't already covered by your webcam." I clear my throat. "Including your private quarters."

Lee's right eyebrow arches. "You want to bug my bedroom?"

"I'm sorry, but yes." Hesitantly, I add: "She may have planted her own bug. Remember, it's happened before."

He winces. His former secretary, Eileen, was a Quorum spy. "Sure, go ahead."

"One last thing." Ack! How do I put this delicately?

"We hope you'll consider wearing special lenses and earbuds. That way, we'll be able to see her exactly from your POV at all times and, um, interrupt if need be."

"You mean if she tries to kill me while we're in bed."

I nod.

"Great, just great. My crush and her entourage want to watch a peep show starring me in case it turns into my snuff act." He rolls his eyes. "Okay, sure. I'll give you your money's worth."

It's my turn to blush. Kyle comes to mind.

Pain darkens Lee's eyes. "I'm sorry, Don. I didn't mean to be so flippant."

I shrug. "It's better to laugh about it than to cry, right?"

"I'll be honest with you: when I make love to her, I think of you."

"Oh, Lee… Really, you shouldn't say—"

"I'm not going to lie to you. And believe me, I had hoped that eventually Lara—or Yelena, or whatever her real name is—would have me feeling differently. That won't happen now. You're stuck with me if only to admire you from afar."

I reach out to touch Lee's face.

He grabs hold of my hand as if it's a lifeline.

Then he kisses my palm.

We stand there, suspended in our grief.

His, from knowing once again he's chosen the wrong woman while regretting that who he thinks is the right one —me—will always be out of reach.

I grieve because I genuinely want my dear friend to be

happy. He'll have to accept that I won't be the one to make that happen.

And it certainly won't be Yelena.

I nod toward the door. "We better get out there before that *Omaha Herald* reporter gets suspicious."

"Not to mention the extremely jealous Mr. Craig," Lee mutters.

Still, he doesn't let go of my hand until we're out of the room.

15

How to Behave When You Are the Guest

Isn't it great when you can take the night off from hosting duties? Don't you find it a relief to relax and let someone else deal with the pressure of being a hostess with the mostess?

What…

You say, "Noooooo!"…?

Oh, dear! If that's how you genuinely feel, it's time for an intervention. Here's how to break free of any anxiety that comes from having no control over any event not of your making:

First, remember your only obligation is to enjoy yourself!

You're to do this even if your hostess's theme is headache-inducing, lacks taste in music, or if the tarnish on her silver gives you cause to shudder. And certainly, don't memorialize your mental checklist of everything she's done wrong. Doing so —even if sent anonymously—will have repercussions! Let's face it: she'll know who's dissing her because of your perfect penmanship and witty turn of phrase.

__Next, even if your hostess's faux pas is abhorrent, you can hone a new skill: acting!__

Start by pretending that you're actually having fun. That's right, turn that frown upside down. Laugh politely at the jokes of others. However, no need to giggle hysterically when something goes terribly wrong at your friend's soirée. Instead, pretend you feel her pain, just as she's done in the past with you.

Wait… All this time, you thought she meant it?

OMG! Like—NO. Give that gal an Academy Award!

__And finally, if all else fails, there's hypnosis.__

No doubt, having someone mesmerize you into thinking that you have no right to set the theme, menu, and guest list, let alone order around the cater-waiters, may seem a drastic step, but it's for your own good. Look at it this way: under such a spell, you're relieved of all obligations to put on a fantastic event! More to the point, you can gossip with everyone else about how your hostess blew her chance to do things right.

"WELL, I'LL BE DAMNED! LEE HAS SURELY GOTTEN HIMSELF IN yet another pickle!"

Jack is crowing so loudly that I have to poke him in the ribs to shut him up. "Keep it down! The Benningtons are right next door!"

Whereas Yelena's suite at Triple L Ranch is next to Lee's.

And yes, she's peeved that Lee invited the Hart Media crew to spend the weekend with them "to get the feel of life after leading the free world."

"Granted, Lee's had his fair share of relationship mistakes. But we've all made them," I counter.

Jack smirks. "Is that the best you can do?"

"Don't act so superior. It's unbecoming."

Jack shrugs. "You're right. Poor Lee. What a sap! He's always falling for femme fatales."

"What about your own infatuation with lethal ladies?" I huff. "Remember your first wife, Valentina?"

"You mean, the one who left me for *your* first husband?" he retorts.

"Yes!... Well, I mean… that's my point exactly!" I exclaim. "We've all been there, done that."

"And yet some of us still crave our vices," he points out.

"What do you mean by that?" I retort. "Once I discovered who Carl really was, I—"

"I'm not talking about you, dear wife," Jack snickers. "Do I have to spell it out? Your boyfriend has questionable taste." He holds up a hand, then counts off with his fingers: "First, there was Babette. Now there's Yelena. And, of course, there's his perennial heartthrob: *you*."

I look skyward. "You're making too much out of this, Jack. And besides, he's not my boyfriend! He's just—*a friend*."

By Jack's sneer, I see he's not buying this line of Grade-A tripe.

"Okay, yeah. Maybe he's got a bit of a crush," I admit. "But his infatuation with me doesn't make me a 'femme fatale.'"

"Don't be so modest. How many men have fallen under your spell—and died because of it?"

All I can do is shrug. "That's a silly question."

"Is that your way of admitting you've lost count?"

"Not at all! It means I do my job well." I sniff. "And as far as Lee is concerned, just because he flirts with me isn't proof that he's in love with me."

Jack stares me down. Finally: "You're lying."

I feel my cheeks flaring. "Why must you be so jealous of Lee?"

"Because he's in love with you—and you know it even though you don't acknowledge it. More to the point, you enjoy it." Jack turns back to the window. Outside, the soft rolling hills are covered with gently mooing cows. "Donna, although it assuages your ego to keep him dangling, if you really care for him—*as a friend*—you'd encourage him to move on."

"You may not want to believe this, but I have clarified that our relationship will always be strictly platonic," I insist.

Jack nods grudgingly. "So, what's lover boy's next move—with Yelena, I mean?"

"This place is even bigger than Lion's Lair, so she'll have a lot of room to do whatever damage she has in mind. Abu and Arnie already have control of Lee's security cameras. Evan is standing by to give tech assistance. By the way, Lee has also agreed to wear Acme lenses while with Yelena in areas that aren't…secure."

"In other words, when they're screwing." Jack smirks. "It's going to be interesting to see if he can get it up now, knowing why she's with him in the first place." Shrugging, he adds, "Worst case scenario: he can close his eyes and pretend he's with you."

Too quickly, I snap, "You're being unnecessarily crude —and cruel!"

"Forgive me, Mrs. Craig, if my barb hit too close to home." Jack stares at me, waiting for me to deny this. I try to speak but don't want to lie to him.

"Thanks for confirming what I'd already suspected." Jack picks up his jacket, heads for the door, but then turns around. "By the way, where is your room?"

"In… another wing," I admit.

"Ah. Got it."

"Oh, come on, Jack! It's not what you think. Lee wants me close in case something goes wrong—"

"No need to explain."

This time when Jack opens the door, it's with a nod for me to take the hint and get lost.

LEE'S ADMINISTRATIVE ASSISTANT, EVE GREEN, IS USHERING Libby, her aides, and her security detail to their own wing of the house. Marcus and Mario go with them. Between now and dinner, they'll play catch-up with POTUS on the rest of our country's and the world's affairs.

As Lee had hoped, our supposed interview gives him a great excuse to dodge 'Lara' between now and dinner. Arnie and Abu join us, ostensibly to light, mic, and record, but really to bug the master suite.

"You say Yelena's room is next door?" Abu asks.

Lee nods. "But she and Mary are busy monitoring the Benningtons' interview with Jack—that is, 'Grant,'—so your team is free to do its thing."

By that, he means bugging her suite too.

They've accomplished this task a quarter-hour later, including the air duct between Lee and Yelena's room.

Triple L's triangular dinner bell rings throughout the grounds. A half-hour ago, menus were slipped under the doors of all occupied suites. Steaks or stream-caught rainbow trout are on the menu, as are mashed potatoes and a summer vegetable bounty. For dessert, the chef has made a cheesecake, a gluten-free chocolate mousse, and s'mores to be served by the campfire.

Lee frowns. He's not looking forward to dinner now that he knows what's what. He's not too anxious to put on a happy face.

I can't say that I blame him.

I take his hand. "Just act normal."

He scoffs. "I don't know what that is anymore."

"As long as she doesn't think you suspect anything, we can catch her in the act and minimize the damage."

He nods. "All the more reason I'm glad I sent the kids and Aunt Phyllis camping. Of course, she hoped I'd send Porter too. But he always wants to be where the action is." Lee looks me in the eye. "If anything is to happen—to me or you—I'd hate for them to see it."

"Or Jack," I add.

Lee shakes his head. "Sure, okay, add Jack to your list."

As opposed to his.

Jack is right. I can't let Lee think he can come between my husband and me.

But right now, I've got a much more important issue to contend with than one's jealousy and the other's idolatry.

If we're going to survive whatever Yelena has planned for us, we've all got to work together to make sure she fails.

Our lives depend on it.

IMAGINE MY SURPRISE WHEN I SEE YELENA IS OUT ON THE veranda—

With Jack.

They sit side by side in Adirondack chairs. Whatever she's saying draws him in so close that she has a hand on his knee.

Make that his thigh.

When they realize that Lee and I are a few feet away, she takes back her hand and then stands up.

Jack rises too. But he doesn't take a step back.

Yelena doesn't seem to mind his close proximity. In fact, she leans into it.

Interesting…

"The Benningtons' interview went well, then?" I try to keep the edge out of my voice.

"Mr. Larkin's time and questions were greatly appreciated by Senator Bennington," Yelena gushes.

"Ah! The usual softballs then, I take it," I mutter.

"Not at all," Yelena demurs. "In fact, Grant came at the

senator pretty hard. He didn't hold anything back and got to the bottom of why we're making an aggressive push toward nuclear armament."

"That's our Grant, alright," I purr. "Coming at you hard. Getting to the bottom of...*whatever*. What a naughty boy he is!"

Jack chuckles. My salaciousness isn't ruffling his feathers.

Yelena's eyes roam from me to him and back to me. She smirks.

"They're holding dinner for us. Shall we head out to the patio?" Lee's voice comes out as a croak.

He's dismayed for all the wrong reasons. Yes, he's worried about being left alone with Yelena.

But he's also miserable because he thinks I care what Jack thinks of her.

Not to worry, friend. Like me, he hates her. It's all part of the game that is our lives in the field—

Which is probably not anywhere close to your own contempt for her.

As we walk outside, Lee takes Yelena's hand.

Good boy.

AN OPEN WHITE BIRCH PERGOLA CROWNS THE SLATE TERRACE. Strands of tiny lights strung throughout its rafters give the grounds a soft, warm glow. We are far enough away from the bright lights of Omaha that the galaxies above us seem close enough to touch in the indigo sky.

The Benningtons have found their places: on either side of Libby, of course, who sits at the head of the large, rough-hewn outdoor table.

Lee takes the table's other end. Yelena sits beside him.

Jack pointedly pulls out the chair on the other side of Lee for me. But instead of taking the seat beside me, he sits beside Yelena.

Eve takes Jack's other side.

Mario plops beside me and whispers, "Your hubby can be harsh."

No one can see my nails dig into Mario's thigh.

He stifles his yelp.

Quizzically, Marcus looks over from where he's sitting: on the other side of Crystal. His scowl says it all: *behave, children.*

A second table has been set up for administrative aides, including Mary. Abu, Arnie, and Evan also sit at this table. Though Mary and Evan pretend they don't know each other, they've managed to sit side by side.

The meal is sumptuous. The conversation is light: about golf, cattle farming, fly fishing.

No talk of politics.

As Libby captivates her end of the table with talk of the best golf courses she's played in the past year of her presidency, Lara looks across the table at me. "You never told us how your interview with Lee went."

Smiling, I glance over at him. "He was very forthcoming. I could have drilled him for at least another hour."

"I'm sure he'd have loved that," Jack mutters.

Lee frowns at him.

Yelena's eyes narrow—first at him, then at Lee. Finally, she says to me: "I've never seen you in the press corps before."

"I usually cover the European beat. But Hart has realized that Grant and I make a great tag team."

"I'll bet," Yelena murmurs.

"So many politicians, too little time." I bat my eyes. "With all the diplomacy Lee has under his belt, I could spend a week lapping up his…wisdom."

Mario chokes on his wine.

This earns him a dirty look from both Marcus and Jack.

Lee covers his laughter with his napkin.

Eve sighs. She's obviously had enough of Yelena and my catcalls because she snaps her fingers at the wait staff, signaling that dessert is to be served.

AFTER A FEW BITES OF MOUSSE, YELENA EXCUSES HERSELF AND walks into the house.

Damn! And all of Acme is sitting out here. She can be doing who-knows-what in there…

Thankfully, she's only gone a few minutes. When she returns, she's joined by two servants wheeling something toward the table. The item is in a large box.

Seeing her, Chad smiles broadly, taps his glass for silence, and then stands. "I'd like to toast our wonderful host, Lee Chiffray."

Everyone cheers and takes a sip.

"I'm also very honored that President Kentfield joined

us in celebrating the implementation of the Global Strike Force. In fact, as a show of gratitude to our Commander in Chief, Crystal and I, along with all the citizens of the great state of Nebraska, wish to honor President Kentfield with this token of our gratitude."

Yelena lifts the box.

Everyone gasps when it reveals an exquisite statue. A cowboy, bronco-busting a grand steed. His hand is held to his brow as if looking off in the distance. Cast in bronze, it's not that big: even with its pedestal, only two feet tall.

"My goodness! It's a Remington!" Libby exclaims.

"There is only one other like it," Chad proudly states. "Crystal and I are donating it to Omaha's Joslyn Art Museum."

Libby tears up. "Crystal…Chad, I'm…tremendously touched! It'll make a great addition to the two other Remingtons already in the White House."

Chad nods at Yelena, who motions to have it wheeled away.

While we linger at the table for another hour, making small talk, Lee breaks out an expensive port.

Soon, though, Libby rises. "We've got a long day tomorrow—beginning with eighteen holes of golf that I've been looking forward to playing since Lee told me his course was originally designed by Jack Nicklaus."

Everyone laughs.

As the party breaks up, Lee reluctantly rises. Before he walks off with Yelena, he looks back at me. When Yelena notices this, she scowls.

"Considering the charm on his arm, why does he look like a man on the way to the electric chair?" Mario muses.

"All in good time, dearie. All in good time," I reply.

He grins. "You're right. Don't tell me until it's all over."

Mary comes over with Evan. "We've got a lot of catching up to do, so we're calling it a night."

"Are you flying back to DC with POTUS tomorrow afternoon?" Jack asks.

Mary nods toward Mario. "He is, as is DNI Branham. But I'm hanging in Nebraska with the Benningtons for another day or two. While they're here, they're meeting with constituents."

"I guess that means Lara is also hanging in?" I ask.

"No. Unfortunately, she just received a text that her terminally ill aunt died this afternoon. She's leaving first thing tomorrow to arrange the funeral."

"Oh…what a shame." Jack and I say together.

Mary stares at me, then Jack. "Why? What's wrong?"

"Nothing," Jack replies.

Mary sighs. "Ah, I get it: need-to-know basis only." She takes Evan's hand. "Come on. You can tell me about all the wild goose chases my parents have put you through, and I'll tell you how boring it is to be a congressional aide."

Evan winces at the offer. Still, he lets her lead him away.

If he's to tell her about Yelena, it will be a real test of their relationship.

Mario salutes us. "Try to stay out of trouble—at least for one night." He walks off with Abu and Arnie, who are rock-paper-scissoring to see who takes the first shift for watching Yelena's moves this evening.

"Your place or mine?" Jack asks.

"It'll have to be mine. I've got to keep an eye on Lee. He's still nervous about having to sleep with the enemy."

Jack cackles at that. "This, I've got to see."

"What...no peep show?" Jack is right. By the time we make it to my room and turn on the monitor, it's obvious that Lee is sleeping alone.

Strange.

Did he blow her off?

Worse yet, did she blow *him* off?

And I don't mean that literally…

Albeit his prone position could be some indication of it…

I murmur, "Arnie, what happened with Lee and Yelena?"

He sighs. "She went in with Lee for a moment, shoved him up against the wall, stripped the buttons off his shirt, and woman-handled him before planting a *very righteous* kiss that practically took the wind out of him. But then she told him she had to leave bright and early tomorrow to catch a plane because her aunt had passed. He seemed surprised but waved her off before flopping down onto the bed. And that's all she wrote."

"Where is she now?" I ask

Silence.

Then: "Are you sure you want to know?"

"Um…YEAH. Give it up."

Arnie sighs. "I was hoping you wouldn't ask. Okay, so: she's waiting outside of Jack's suite."

Jack raises his hands as a declaration of innocence.

Ah. Well.

"I guess the best man won," I declare. When Jack puts his hand on my arm, I shrug it off. "A gentleman never keeps a lady waiting."

At least he has the decency to kiss me goodbye first.

I stifle the urge to bite his lip so that he winces each time she kisses him.

I'm about to turn off the monitor, but something stops me. I'm thinking of how Lee looked, passed out on his bed.

I switch to that feed. Fully dressed other than his unbuttoned shirt, he's down for the count.

Arnie is right: the stress of having to fake it with Yelena must have exhausted him.

Still, he got off lightly compared to Jack. I've got eyes and ears on him and Yelena through his lenses. I can't stomach what I see: my husband is undressing the woman ruining my summer.

I turn off the monitor.

Then I turn it on again, but this time switching back to Lee's room.

He still hasn't moved out of the bed.

Something isn't right. He's dead to the world…

I run into his room.

❧

I'M STILL PUMPING LEE'S CHEST AND GIVING MOUTH-TO-mouth when Abu rushes in. He has a syringe in his hand. A moment later, the needle is in Lee's chest.

The next thing I know, Lee is gasping…

And upchucking.

"What did you give him?" I ask Abu.

"Digibind," he replies. "He had a heart attack. My guess is Yelena gave him something that caused it."

"But when?" I ask. "At dinner—in his food or a drink? I don't see how because that would have meant a delayed effect…"

And now she's with Jack.

If she's somehow recognized him from these missions…

I run out of my room and all the way to Jack's suite.

SHE'S STRADDLING JACK AND MOANING SO ECSTATICALLY THAT she doesn't hear me enter the room.

From behind, I grab her hair with my left hand. Before she knows it, I slash her throat with the other.

Her death rattle lasts just a few seconds before she drops onto the bed like a rag doll.

Jack shoves her away before leaping out of bed. *"Donna —what the hell?"*

"She tried to kill Lee just now," I explain. "She made it look like a heart attack. They wouldn't have found him until the morning. By then, she would have been long gone —quote-unquote out of town to arrange her aunt's funeral." I toss Jack his pants.

As he slips them on, he declares, "I guess I was supposed to be her alibi." He reaches for his shirt but stops: "Her mission couldn't have been to kill Lee. That would make no sense."

Shite. He's right.

I sigh. "I guess now we'll never know what it was."

"We'd better find out because it's still in play," Jack replies. "Otherwise, we've failed at ours."

Ah hell. He's right.

16

Readying a Guest Room

An accommodating hostess never minds overnight guests! ...

Okay, maybe sometimes. But a hostess's reputation rises and falls on how they are treated before her guests leave her luxurious home.

Preferably, not in a pine box.

To ensure this is never the case, here are a few tips:

First, make the stay as comfortable as possible.

A room with a view? What a great touch! A breakfast smorgasbord? How generous! A nightly turn-down service and chocolates on the pillow? How sweet! Your guests may never want to leave...

Which ain't the point.

Solution: have a few signature touches, but never go overboard—

Unless they're great tippers.

Next, keep them entertained.

By that, I mean taking them on tours to renowned local sites and involving them in inspiring activities. Hopefully, you live somewhere they'll feel going to is a one-and-done so that it doesn't become an annual pilgrimage. If it turns out to be the latter, buy a cross and nail them to it.

Oh, and one last thing: make the terms of the stay crystal clear.

Indeed, you've heard that old canard: "fish and visitors stink after three days." No, you haven't? Spoiler alert: IT'S TRUE. Three days seems about right. Whatever terms you agree to, get it in writing. It will stand up better in court when you go for a process server.

(Tip: If you go for a shotgun, the written agreement probably won't help much.)

"LET ME GET THIS STRAIGHT: THE WOMAN YOU KNOW AS LARA invited herself into your suite, gave you a deep, soul-searing kiss, then begged off from having sex because she had an early plane to catch, only to go into my room and ride me like a bronco buster?" Jack shakes his head as if he's genuinely awed. "Dude, for real: you're not that hard up that just looking at her gave you a heart attack. Don't you remember anything?"

Lee stares out his door—which Eve insists should stay open so that his Secret Service detail can monitor him through the night—before turning back to glare at Jack. "Whereas your boyish charms work wonders on women who threaten our national security." Lee rubs his forehead with both hands. "It wasn't just a kiss, though."

"We've, um, seen the video footage," I point out.

I play it for him.

Afterward, I say, "From what we can tell, she shoved you against the wall, then tore at the buttons on your shirt."

Jack nods at Lee. "Somehow, you turned her off cold turkey. Maybe it was your breath?"

Fists clenched, Lee takes a step toward him. "Quit baiting me. All I remember is… is a quick, sharp pain… to my chest."

I move next to Lee. His shirt, still unbuttoned, leaves his chest exposed. He allows my hand to roam through the curly rug of hair between his nipples. When I reach the skin over his heart, he flinches.

I lean in, scrutinizing it. "Jack, take a look at this!"

He sighs. "Must I?"

"Quit being an ass." I shove his head downward so he's at eye level with Lee's nipple. "Right there! See that tiny dot, and the other beside it? One was courtesy of Yelena. Possibly Digitalis. The other was made by Abu: Digibind, to save Lee's life."

Grudgingly, Jack nods. "I guess Unit 29155 has moved away from pricking its enemies with nerve agents to ones that give an instant heart attack. Makes sense. Less detectable and a quicker death."

"It's a much smaller needle too. The GRU has certainly perfected its kill-poke," I point out.

Jack muses, "As we've also found out—unfortunately —a spray bottle can be hit or miss—"

"Who gives a shit?" Lee stalks the room. "Have you two forgotten that I almost died?"

"You would have been sorely missed." Jack's smirk undermines his words.

The next thing I know, Lee is pummeling Jack.

Lee's Secret Service detail bursts into the room. Eve, Marcus, and Mario are on their heels.

Porter and his team pull their boss off my husband, but not before Lee's fists have done some real damage: Jack is now sporting a shiner.

"The doctor is here," Eve tells Lee. "He's setting up in the examination room."

"Perfect timing," Lee mutters. Buttoning up his shirt, he turns to Jack. "Feel free to leave at any time." He spits out the words as if they're nails.

"Her too?" Jack points at me.

"No. Donna is always welcome—*wherever I am.*" Lee walks out.

Before Porter follows, he shrugs at Jack. "So much for my best man getting along with one of my groomsmen."

Eve takes Jack's hand. Wiping away a tear on her cheek, she whispers, "Lee will cool off. Just give him time."

"I guess I was a bit rough on him," Jack admits.

"This helped him get it out of his system." Gently, she touches his shiner. "Let's do what we can to take it easy on him tonight. He almost died, remember?"

She closes the door behind her.

"She's the one he should be pining for," Jack declares. "Do you see the way she looks at him?"

"You're right," I admit. "And it would certainly make my life easier."

"You two don't have time to play Cupid," Marcus huffs. "We still don't know what Yelena was up to while she was here."

"This place has, what, a thousand rooms? I can still work in the shadows. Lee won't even know I'm here," Jack insists.

"If you feel that way, then I'd suggest that your team fit you up with a different face and that you don't do anything stupid that makes our host want to wallop the other eye." Marcus isn't joking.

"Are POTUS and the Benningtons to know that Yelena met with an accident?" I ask him.

"Certainly not!" He shudders. "As far as they're concerned, it's business as usual. Otherwise, it'll scuttle all of Acme's hard work."

"But won't the senator wonder why he can't reach out to his aide when she doesn't answer his calls or texts, let alone why she's never coming back from the funeral?" Jack insists.

Marcus frowns but says nothing for the longest time. Finally: "Yelena wasn't the only mole. She was working in tandem with someone else."

"Why weren't we told this?" Jack asks.

"Two reasons. First of all, she was the bagman. You did your job admirably: shadowing her and counter-sabotaging her efforts. Not that we want her handler to know it."

"And Reason Number Two?" Jack prods.

"We were hoping to flip her to our side," Marcus admits. "Doable, if we'd divulged how at every step she'd been undermined—and that Russia would blame her for her failures. Or worse yet, that the Russians might conclude she'd already been turned and knew she was passing them faulty intel. They'd know that giving up her handler would have been the only way she could negotiate her way out of immediate deportation and make an offer for Witness Protection."

"In other words, she'd be rewarded by our country despite all of the lives she's ruined!" I retort. "That's…ludicrous!"

"It's a moot point now," Marcus reminds me. "And you've still got a big feat ahead of you: figuring out the last mission Yelena set into motion."

He takes his leave.

"Let's go search Yelena's room for clues." I nod toward the door that adjoins Lee's. "When we leave, we'll sneak out her front door. Lee won't even see us because it faces a different hall."

I don't have to ask twice.

"Before dinner, Arnie and Abu were manning the security feeds," Jack reminds me as he rummages through

Yelena's dresser. "If she was surreptitious in any way, they would have picked up on it."

I look up from her suitcase, which I'm checking for hidden compartments. "Everyone went outside when dinner was served." Suddenly it comes to me: "But during dessert, she went inside to get the gift for POTUS. No one was manning the cameras then."

Jack reaches for his cell to call Arnie.

A moment later, our tech op is combing through the footage of Yelena's trek through Triple L. "She went into one of the huge walk-in closets off the reception area," Arnie confirms. After a few computer clicks, he adds: "There is no security camera in the closet. And I'm sorry to say, we didn't think of putting one in there. However, from her phone logs, I can tell that she was sent a text while she was there. The transmission came from a phone belonging to 'C Bennington.'"

"Well, that makes sense since she was retrieving the gift Chad gave POTUS," Jack says.

"What did he text her?" I ask.

"All it says is 'TO+15,'" Arnie replies.

"Perhaps the congressman asked her to look something up for him when she went inside," I suggest.

"If that were the case, the footage shows she didn't go anywhere else or use a device to look up anything," he tells us. "Next, she wrangled two wait staff to wheel the gift outside. She stayed right on their heels."

"She didn't have her cell when she jumped my bones, so it must still be here somewhere," Jack reasons.

Arnie snorts. "She keeps it in the bottom dresser drawer among her, um, unmentionables."

Jack pulls the cell out of the drawer with a handful of colorful thongs and bras. "Well hidden, but just a momentary deterrent for any thief who wants to find it."

"So glad the search hasn't left you all giddy." I snatch it from him. "Arnie, what's her passcode?"

He reads it to me but adds, "From what I can tell, other than that one text and some light flirting between her and Lee, she had no other correspondence since she arrived at Triple L."

"Then whatever she set into motion must have happened earlier." I pace the room, frustrated. "We must be missing something! POTUS is here until fifteen hundred tomorrow. Then POTUS, her aides, and Marcus and Mario fly back to DC. Arnie: you, Evan, and Abu will go over every inch of camera footage from when Yelena stepped onto Triple L until she died. We've got to figure out what she did and when she did it."

"On it," he vows. "By the way, Jack: Abu has completed the wet work in your room. You're free to go back there. It'll certainly be far enough away from Lee that it won't give him palpitations again." He signs off.

Jack sighs. "How do you feel about that?"

I shiver. "To be honest, it creeps me out."

"I hear you." Jack frowns. "Well then…I guess there's always your room."

"It's on the other side of Lee's. Remember?" I nod in the direction of the adjoining door.

Jack walks over to it and peeks in. "He's not back from

the examination room. If you want, we can slip right in from here. He'll never even know we're there."

"Not too close for comfort, should, you know, we feel frisky?" I tease.

"You're right. Considering you're a screamer, it may be too risky."

I smack his arm. "You wish. Come on, let's make a break for it."

As it is, because the day has been exhausting enough— not to mention Triple L's bed is fit for royalty—we pass out as soon as our heads hit their pillows.

At eight in the morning, the gentle buzz of my cell wakes me. "Wake up, sleepyheads. Ryan wants to give you the bad news in person." Abu's tone is light enough.

I nudge Jack, who grunts but sits up straight. "What is it?" he croaks.

I put my cell phone on speaker mode: "Go ahead, Ryan. The gang's all here."

"Abu, why don't you start?" Ryan says.

"To be honest, there's not much to give." Abu sighs. "We went through every bit of footage, beginning when Yelena showed up after the Offutt AFB event with the rest of Lee's entourage and until Donna's—well, for lack of a better word, 'surprise visit.'"

"We'll just have to assume that whatever her game plan was, it died with her," I reason.

"I suggest we stay alert until POTUS is wings up,"

Ryan declares. "Unfortunately, Jack's altercation with Lee puts us a man down."

"Maybe I should have a talk with Lee," I suggest.

"I'm sure he'd love to see you grovel on my behalf," Jack grumbles.

"She wouldn't have to do it if you'd kept your lip zipped," Ryan growls. "Donna, make nice with your host."

"I'll get right on it," I reply.

Ryan signs off.

"Lousy double-entendre, wife," Jack mutters.

"Quit reading something from nothing," I warn him.

Jack apologizes with a sweet, deep kiss.

Yep, he's forgiven.

ABU DOES QUICK WORK IN MAKING ME UP AS GWENDOLYN. AS I scrutinize his handiwork in the mirror, I exclaim, "You're almost as good as that Hollywood make-up artist everyone's talking about: Donna Levy."

Flattered, Abu bows. "That's heavy praise! I wonder if she'd take me on as an apprentice?"

I laugh. "You really are tired of working for Acme, aren't you?"

He shrugs. "The wet work gets a bit tiresome. And, quite frankly, I've got to admit what you did to Yelena had me thinking twice about going into the pie business with you. Let's just say I'd never want to cross you." Noting my scowl, he adds: "Hey, watch the frown lines!" He picks up a tiny brush from Gwendolyn's make-up palette and smooths out a crease.

"Trust me, I'm not offended," I mutter. "To prove it, I'm gifting you my cherry pie recipe in my will."

His laugh comes out as a sputter. "Well, hell, girl! Then I'll never see it. You're like a cat with nine lives."

"One never knows. But I'm doing my best to stay in the game of Life. I have too much to lose, starting with my three children."

"And a loving husband." Lee's voice has me turning around.

"Yes, that he is." I sit up in my chair.

Not wanting to be the third wheel, Abu nods and walks out.

Lee sits beside me. "I never got to thank you for saving my life."

I blush. "If I remember correctly, you've done the same for me occasionally. Should we call it even?"

"Never. I'll always be in your debt—on many levels for many reasons."

"That's why we're best friends," I reply.

"I know that. I also realize… I now know it's all we will ever be." Lee picks up my hand and squeezes it. "I'm sorry I let Jack get under my skin."

"And I'm sorry he was a big enough ass to do it. By the way, he'd like to apologize, but he doesn't want to get shot by your Secret Service detail."

Lee chuckles. "In that case, I'll tell them to stand down but stand by." He nods grudgingly. "I'll accept his apology on one condition: that he accepts mine as well."

"That shiner did ruin that pretty face of his." I have to smile.

"To be honest, that isn't why I'd be apologizing to him." Lee looks away. "I should have never confessed my unrequited love for you. It put you in a difficult spot: yet again, you had to put me in my place. Whether you mentioned it to Jack or not, he obviously knows it and resents it—as I would too if the shoe were on the other foot." He turns to face me. "Donna, you—and Jack—have my solemn promise that I'll do what I can to keep my feelings for you to myself. I'd never want to lose your friendship over it, or for that matter, Jack's. That is if he'll accept mine again."

"Why don't you ask him yourself?" I nod toward the door to my room.

He hesitates. Finally, he walks toward it and knocks.

Jack opens it. He's wary enough to take a step back.

I'm tempted to see the male version of kissing and making up, but my appetite has gotten the better of me, so I head to the dining room.

ONLY MARY, EVAN, MARIO, AND MARCUS ARE DIGGING into breakfast. "Lee and 'Grant' should be down soon," I inform them. "Is POTUS ready to hit the links?"

"There's been a change in plans," Mary informs me. "If we're to avoid another government shutdown, the Senate needs all hands on deck today to vote on its approval. In a couple of hours, I'll be flying back to DC after all—with Senator and Mrs. Bennington."

My face falls. I'd hoped to have a little more time with Mary.

Apparently, Evan feels the same way because his smile has disappeared.

"Excuse me… What did you just say?" Chad Bennington's voice comes from behind me.

His face has lost all its color.

On the other hand, Libby shows her frustration by hitting the wall with her open hand.

"Sorry, Madame President—and sir—but it's true," Mary replies. "As a courtesy, I've already sent a text to Lara. Though mourning, she'll want to know about the schedule change. Not that she was going to meet us in Omaha for the town meetings—"

"But.. I… I can't go back to DC," Chad insists.

"Why not?" I ask sweetly.

Chad smirks at my doe-eyed innocence. "My dear wife's parents are celebrating their 50th wedding anniversary tomorrow. There's no way either of us is going to miss that." He frowns at Mary. "You keep her calendar. You should know that."

"I…" Flustered, Mary taps her iPad. Staring at it, she murmurs, "Yes, sir. Sorry. I see it right here."

Libby rolls her eyes. "Ah, heck! And I was so looking forward to playing that back nine. There goes my chance to win back the last sawbuck I lost to Lee." She taps Chad on the shoulder. "Sorry, Senator. You'll have to postpone the hometown coffee klatches. Government shutdowns wait for no man or woman. You and Crystal can hitch a ride back with the rest of us."

"Senator, I'll call the Omaha office so that they can formalize the cancellations of your appointments," Mary pipes up.

"No… *don't*! I'll… I'll do that myself." He shrugs. "Instead, go break the news to my wife. I've got some things to attend to."

Mary bites her lower lip and then nods. "Yes, sir."

Chad follows Libby and her team down the hall.

Mary's got a strange look on her face. "What's up?" I ask.

She frowns. "What he said isn't true. Crystal's parents' fiftieth wedding anniversary party isn't until next month. I know because I helped make the party arrangements." She leaps up. "In any regard, I'd better tell Mrs. Bennington of this change in their schedule." She's out of the room in a flash.

Mario hoots. "Told you, sir!"

Sighing, Marcus hands Mario a five-dollar bill.

Mario snaps it and checks the watermark. "Real enough."

Evan grins at their antics.

"What was that all about?" I ask. Suddenly, it comes to me: "Oh, I get it. You think Bennington is the other mole. Am I right?"

Mario nods. "And if so, he's already done immense damage. To have a foreign adversary infiltrate such a high level of government—*and for all these years*—"

"If we're right, he'll spend the rest of his life in a

Federal prison," Marcus replies. "If we're wrong, he's got the power to decimate all eighteen agencies of the US Intelligence Community." He leans in: "Which is why, Mrs. Craig, you can't blow the stunt we're now asking you to pull."

I groan. "Okay, what is it?"

Mario leans in. "Since your interview with Lee, Chad has been eyeing you like a juicy slice of Triple L's char-broiled chateaubriand."

In other words, you want me to get personal with him." The thought makes me shudder.

"Affirmative. We need you to ask the senator for an interview so that you can plant a bug on him." He holds up a SIM card. "Replace the one in his cell phone with this one. Whether by phone or in person, we'll be able to hear every conversation."

"He's got a plane to catch," I remind him. "What if he says he can't make the time?"

Mario, Evan, and Marcus exchange glances.

Marcus replies. "According to Acme reconnaissance, that call he had to make was to his mistress—the aide who runs his Omaha office—to let her know he won't be seeing her. Unfortunately, he's blue-pilled up and ready to pop. The last thing he wants is to take a three-hour plane ride with no one to take to the Mile-High Club, so...."

"I get it. I'm to be the sacrificial lamb." I go nose to nose with Evan: "Not a word to Mary about this."

Red-faced, he crosses his heart.

17

Bad Manners

---

*W*HAT SHOULD YOU DO ABOUT IMPOLITE GUESTS?

If you assume you should just bite your tongue and cross off their names from future party lists, I firmly insist that you DON'T STOP THERE.

Instead, lead by example. Ask them politely to defer from further bad behavior. Hopefully, they won't ignore you.

However, if they still insist on acting like spoiled brats, get out the whip—

Not figuratively, silly goose! Literally! The taste of the lash never fails to achieve the desired results.

EVEN LEE'S THICK ORNATE DOORS CAN'T MUFFLE THE argument from the Benningtons' suite. I bow to temptation and put my ear to it.

Crystal is growling: "—to DC by yourself. I'm staying in Omaha."

"But honeybun, you know we've got to show a united front back in the District!"

"I've already told you—*I'm not going!* If you're so anxious to have a little company, feel free to give my seat to your little whore—"

Ah! So she knows about Yelena…

Well, she's got nothing to worry about on that front…

Just then, she swings the door open. Before she realizes I'm there, I catch my footing. "Knock, knock, dear Benningtons! I was hoping to catch the senator for a quick interview—if he can make the time, that is."

Grinning, Chad stands up straight—as much as he can, considering his obvious boner. I guess Marcus was right about his Vita-Meata-Vegamin. At least, the "meat" part.

Crystal smirks, "He's all yours, duchess. Just don't make him miss his flight." She stalks off.

"But… *honey lamb!*" Chad's plea is feeble, as is his attempt to stop her. He only gets as far as the doorway, which puts us too close for comfort, as far as I'm concerned.

Especially when he pats my backside. "Come on in and make yourself at home." To prove he means business, he shoves me over to the bed and pulls me down onto it beside him.

"I dare say I've never done an interview lying down," I reply.

"There's a first time for everything." His hand wiggles up my skirt.

I slap it away. "Business before pleasure."

"Tell you what." He looks me up and down—and drools. "We'll play a little game. Every answer I give you comes with a price."

"I never pay for interviews," I sniff.

"How badly do you want it?"

"Well, I… I had promised my editor an exclusive with the head of the Senate Subcommittee on Strategic Forces." I sigh as if defeated. "What's the price?"

"How about you take off something for each question I answer?" He tweaks a button on my blouse. "Let's start with this wispy little thing."

"Well… Okay—but only if you shed something too." I lick my lips to signal my anticipation.

In truth, the thought of this game is triggering my gag reflex.

Chad guffaws. "Well, now—this is going to be fun!"

From my bra, I pull a tiny pad with the SIM card between its pages. Batting my eyes, I purr, "Shall we get started?"

SENATOR BENNINGTON HAS A TRULY FASCINATING TAKE ON nuclear disarmament. Of course, I have to doff my skirt to hear it.

At the same time, he lets his lucky plaid golf pants drop to his ankles.

By now, I've already shed my blouse (to Chad's

delight), my scarf, both earrings, and a necklace (to his impatient chagrin).

I'm down to bra and panties.

The one saving grace is that Chad does love to hear himself talk. He thinks my fascination with his pearls of wisdom is due to his place of power.

All I can think of is changing out that SIM card and getting the hell outta here.

"Senator, tell me: what is your biggest fear about Russia?" I ask. Before he can answer, I jerk off his boxers, push him back down on the bed, roll him over onto his stomach, and tie his hands to his legs behind him with his belt.

As I tie my scarf over his eyes, he opines, "Well, now, er… this just got interesting!"

"Keep talking world domination," I purr. "It's such a turn-on!"

NOT.

I straddle him backward and massage his back. He groans ecstatically as one of my hands roams down to his rump.

The other is reaching for the phone.

Between his blather about growing fascism in Europe and how Russia's one cudgel—its oil reserves—is the carrot it holds over Europe, I'm able to replace the SIM card;

And Chad is excited enough to expel onto the bedspread what the little blue pill has wrought.

He sighs. Relief comes with his output, if not the outcome he'd hoped for.

Well, too bad. To rub it in, I purr, "Was it as good for you as it was for me?"

Undeterred, he opines hopefully, "Hey, how about a threesome next time? Say, you, me, and that pretty new aide on my staff… What's her name again? Oh yeah—Mary. She strikes me as game for anything."

I freeze.

Has she and he…

No, of course not! …

But what if she has? What if her anger at me has caused her to act out?

What if he's seen her vulnerability and coerced her into…this?

How.

Dare.

He!

The scarf I've tied over his eyes is long enough to wrap both ends around his neck and tie it to the bedposts while sweet-talking him about a bit of a surprise I've got for him.

Then I pull on the scarf.

This is a first for me: asphyxiation. I'll make sure it's the last time Chad tries it.

I wonder how long it'll take before he passes out—

Or better yet, dies. The more he struggles, the tighter it gets.

How dare he sully my daughter…

He's still gasping when I hear behind me: "What the hell is going on here?"

I turn around to find Mary staring at us from the foot of the bed.

Her shock wears off before mine. She scoops up my clothes and tosses them at me. "Please just… *leave!*"

She does the same with Chad.

To dress, I must let loose of the scarf.

What a shame.

Still hog-tied, it takes Chad a while to choke out, "Hey, we were just talking about you! Want to join the fun?"

I see the temptation in Mary's eyes: to grab the scarf and yank it with all her might.

Instead, she runs out the door—

Past her boss: Crystal, whose glare would melt an Arctic glacier.

When her eyes light on me, it certainly sends a chill down my spine.

Chad feels it too—and it's not just because he's naked except for the scarf and belt that keeps him trussed so tightly that all he can do is roll off the bed to stop his wife as she walks away.

IT TAKES ME ALL OF A MINUTE TO GET DRESSED.

By then, Mary has run up the stairs to her room.

I'm right on her heels.

When she gets to the end of the long hallway, she fumbles with her key but can't open the door quickly enough to slam it in my face.

I follow her inside and shut it behind me.

"Why him?" Mary has tears in her eyes.

"I had to do it! He's a person of interest." Hesitantly, I add, "Please level with me: has he…and you…."

She backs away, disgusted. "Mother! How could you think such a thing?"

"He wanted to… And he implied that you… well…"

Mary looks up, shocked. "And you believed him?"

"Sometimes those in powerful positions have a certain charisma—"

"Trust me, he's got nothing but a dirty mouth and fast hands—and on numerous occasions, I've threatened him to keep both away from me. Well, now I don't have to put up with it!"

Thank goodness! …

But, of course, she has. I reach out to her. "Look…what you saw in there—"

"Crystal is kind and sweet and caring!" She's shaking so hard that her voice trembles: "I feel so…so *sad* for you right now!"

"Mary, you know what I do for a living… and what I sometimes have to do because of it."

"Still, it doesn't mean I like to think of you like—*that.*" Tears run down her cheeks. "*My God!* How does Dad put up with it?"

I shrug. "Sometimes he has to…he has to do it too."

Adamantly, she shakes her head. "I could never live like that. And neither can Evan. He told me so just last night."

I nod. "His decision is sound. As he's learned the hard way, if you're going to be in the field…well, it comes with the territory. I'm so glad he leveled with you about what happened…"

Seeing the look on her face, I stop.

"Who? … *Evan?*" Mary stares at me.

Oh…

Heck!

He never told her about Yelena.

Mary can read my face, too.

She runs out of the room.

I'm about to run after her when my phone buzzes:

It's Jack.

I'm about to speak, but he beats me to the punch: "Donna, meet us in your room as soon as you can. It's about Dominic."

Oh…

No.

"I'm on my way," I whisper.

————————————————

18

Sleepover Parties

————————————————

*E*VERY *PARENT HAS HAD A CHILD BEGGING FOR A SLEEPOVER
party. Despite your reservations, yes, you should give in to the
request. Here's why:*

*First, who knows how lackadaisical other parents may be
when supervising a houseful of rambunctious preteens? It's the
best way to keep an eye on your special little prince or princess.
(And besides, any other mother with a houseful of caterwauling
kids would be drinking a heck of a lot more than you... right?)*

*Next, you can scope out the group's troublemakers, degener-
ates, and reprobates and isolate them so that they don't hurt—or
worse yet, influence—your precious child. Besides, the earlier
they learn their place in a chain gang, the better.*

*And finally: setting yourself as the designated sleepover
house guarantees your child's popularity all the way to college!
Does it really matter if roving armies of teens are trampling your
bushes, trashing your house, decimating your liquor cabinet, and*

using your bedrooms as make-out havens? Of course not! Your precious darling will always have an entourage.

And that's all that matters.

I OPEN THE DOOR TO MY SUITE TO FIND MARCUS, ARNIE, Mario, and Abu there with Jack.

Evan is nowhere to be found. I assume he's getting reamed out by Mary.

The monitor is on. Ryan sits beside an empty hospital bed.

I brush away the tears rolling down my cheeks—

Until I see Jody. She's pushing a wheelchair.

Dominic is in it.

He winces as he props himself up. Still, his strength of spirit proves itself in his broad smile and stoic gaze.

"I'm sure you've missed me," he says.

"We have indeed," I reply.

"Most of all, because you're the best comic relief," Jack teases.

"I believe it. My antics have a habit of putting tears in Donna's eyes." He winks at me.

As I laugh at this joke at my expense, Dominic taps his fist to his heart. It seems he's looking right at me.

I do the same.

"Dominic's energy is lagging, but he has something important to say." Jody's tone is firm.

"As always, my personal nurse is spot on. I seem to tire easily." He pats her hand. "I'll be quick and to the point with my recap of the event that put me here." He takes a deep breath. "When I sprayed Acme's Love Potion on Myrna, and she fainted, I thought it best to make her lie down. It was foolish of me to carry her there. Because I let my guard down, she was able to grab the gun in my back holster, which is why I am sidelined now." He sighs. "Needless to say, it could have been a lot worse. We all know that."

Jody kisses his forehead.

"It's only this past hour I remembered something that may be useful to the mission." Dominic leans closer to the monitor. "As Myrna shot me, the last thing she said was something to the effect of 'I know Stepan sent you to kill me now that Crystal is doing his dirty work.'"

"*Crystal?*" Our response is a Greek chorus of shock.

"That makes sense. Having been stationed at Offutt, Myrna would have been in contact with the senator and his wife," I point out.

"Emma, play the video from Dominic's lenses and the feed from the covert video cams. Let's see if what he heard is what Myrna says," Ryan commands.

Emma does as she's told:

We see Dominic already at the elevator. Just as Myrna gets her room card from the front desk, he pushes the button to her floor. When she asks that he hold the elevator, he acquiesces, even asking her which floor she'd like. When Myrna gets in, she notices he's already pushed her elevator floor. To eat up time, she fidgets with her bags.

That's when he spritzes her.

To test the drug's effectiveness, Dominic asks Myrna a

test question: if she'll allow him to wheel her bag to her room. She murmurs her thanks.

Once she opens the door, she also allows him to follow her in;

When he lifts the suitcase onto the desk, his joke about it containing a dead body is met with complete sincerity as to its actual content.

So, yes, she's deep in a trance…

Until he asks her when she'll be meeting with Bychkov.

Suddenly, she faints.

He catches her before she falls.

As he carries her toward the bed, she comes to with a start. Then she reaches around to the small of his back and grabs the pistol there.

Dominic jerks forward when shot, dropping her. He's shouting in pain. At the same time, she's talking over him, crying, and panicking. Suddenly she picks up the gun again–

And shoots herself in the head.

Shivering, Dominic passes out.

"Emma, rewind to where she's talking," I suggest. "Maybe we can make out what she's saying."

Emma does this, but Dominic's shouts drown out Myrna's words.

He's praying that he doesn't die.

He's calling out for Jody.

Now Jody is crying. So that Dominic doesn't see this, she walks out of the room.

"Rewind, only this time without the sound—and do it in slow motion," I implore.

Emma acquiesces. We watch it again:

I see her form the words:

Stepan sent you to kill me, eh? Okay then, his whore, Crystal, can do his dirty work.

Though he's still praying aloud, Dominic closes his eyes before she blows out her brains.

Ryan sighs. "That's enough."

I say the words I saw formed by her lips.

"ComInt has lip-reading software that can confirm," Emma replies. "But, yeah, that's what it looked like to me too."

"ComInt should also narrow down the GPS on the cell phone we assume belonged to Chad," I point out. "They were sitting close together but not next to each other. They were on either side of POTUS."

"I'll get on that," Arnie declares.

"By the way, we were able to assess the true identity of Yelena," Emma informs us. "Her real name is Mila Levedeva. She was trained as a gymnast but sidelined after an injury, at which point she joined Russia's foreign intelligence service's Directorate KR."

"Where she learned enough counter-intelligence to acquire a clean paper trail and be embedded as a US senator's aide," I point out.

"Levedeva, eh? In Russian, the word means 'swan.'" Arnie snickers. "Yeah, she sang her swan song, thanks to Donna."

"Quit showing off your preschool knowledge of

Russia's animal kingdom," Jack retorts. "We've got more important things to find out—like what "TO+15" stands for."

Yelena's swan song…

A cold chill runs up my spine.

"I think I know!" I exclaim. "But to be sure, we'll have to set a trap for Crystal…."

AN HOUR LATER, I KNOCK ON THE DOOR OF CRYSTAL'S SUITE. Like everyone else, I know that Chad has been banished to any other room but that one.

Like the rest of the DC delegation's, his luggage is waiting to be loaded onto the plane.

Not Crystal's. She's holding firm to her declaration that she's staying in Omaha.

In fact, her car is already packed. She had Mary supervising the task.

When I show up to request a meeting with Crystal, Mary bars the door. With a trembling voice, Mary declares: "She has no desire to see the woman who… *seduced her husband!*"

"You know well that's not the case. She's caught that man whore in so many compromising positions that she should be used to it by now! In fact, you should know that she's—"

"Mary! Who's at the door?" Crystal growls.

"It's…" Mary doesn't know how to answer "Ms. Durant?"

"That homewrecking slut?" Mary's head swivels from where her boss is standing then to me.

So that she understands I'm not offended, I pretend to play a tiny violin.

Exasperated, Mary shakes her head but turns to answer Crystal: "The one and the same. Shall I tell her you're predisposed?"

Silence.

Finally, Crystal announces, "I'll speak to her—"

Mary shrugs as I move past her and into the suite.

"—alone. You may pack and get ready to leave."

"Yes, ma'am. As requested, Mr. Chiffray has put a car at our disposal. He'll send someone tomorrow to drive it back to Triple L."

"You're not going to Omaha with me, Mary. You're to accompany my soon-to-be ex-husband back to DC. You'd better hurry. The plane is taking off in less than an hour. Run along and pack."

Mary is slack-jawed at Crystal's declaration. "But… *why*? Mrs. Bennington, I told you his lasciviousness was just as offensive to me as it was to you—"

"How dare you say such a thing?" Crystal holds up her hand as if genuinely offended. "I'm sorry, but no! You're an ambitious, pretty little thing. I don't hold that against you. But I can't assume that someone my husband is practically salivating over will always be loyal to me when the true power lies with him. Good luck, Mary. You'll need it."

Upset, Mary walks out of the room. Still, she holds her head high.

Turning her back on my daughter, Crystal goes to her

make-up table. Her teary demeanor is now a smug smirk. She stares into her mirror while applying her lipstick. "We'll have our little chat now, Gwendolyn. I'll give you five minutes to grovel, but I'll make no promises that I won't call Hart Media and have them kick your plump ass out the door."

PLUMP?...

The nerve of her!

And then I notice that she's left her purse on the nightstand.

"I just want to apologize for the uncompromising position you found me in with your husband." My tone is contrite. Slowly I move toward the purse. Putting it behind my back, I open it, rummage inside—

Yep, here's her cell phone.

"It wasn't the first time I've caught him in bed with a slattern like you—but it will certainly be the last." As Crystal examines a frown line, I open the back and slip out the SIM card. "In a way, you've done me a favor," she continues. "I should have divorced him long ago. When I tell Hart Media that I'm naming one of their star reporters as a co-defendant, I'm sure they'll pay me handsomely to keep my mouth shut."

She's now staring at me through her mirror. I give her what she's looking for: a defeated sigh. "I assume you're right. And I also assume it means the end of your husband's political career, what with his squeaky-clean pro-family platform."

My declaration has her laughing so hard that she has to put her mascara brush away. "You're right about that, hon! He *will not* have his Congressional seat much longer."

As she goes back to darkening her lashes, I slip her phone—now activated with Acme's SIM card—back into her purse.

"Maybe the citizens in your district will see you as a better replacement," I suggest. I pause as if a thought just came to me: "But…that only happens when a politician dies in office, right? As a courtesy to the widow—who always toes the party line?"

Her eyes seek out mine again through the mirror, but I smile sweetly. Finally, she shrugs. "Sure, it's happened before—*but not only for that reason.* Our constituents love me. Once I spill the beans on his whoremongering—and yours—I'll have their sympathy and their vote. And I'd certainly be the lesser of two evils."

I can't help but laugh. "If you say so!"

She tosses a brush at me but misses.

I'm still chuckling as I go out the door.

Jack is waiting for me in my suite—

But not Mary.

I hide my disappointment with a shrug. "Was it as I thought—a bomb secreted in the statue?"

"No, sorry. No hidden compartments. To make sure, we also put it through the x-ray machine. The base was solid wood, and the statue was solid bronze."

"Ah! … Well, I guess I was wrong." I frown. "Was

everyone's luggage checked too—especially Chad's? Crystal was pretty adamant that he go back to DC with POTUS."

"Sorry to disappoint, but besides a few sex toys in a secret compartment, Chad came clean, as did all the other luggage," Jack replies. "The plane had a thorough going-over too."

"Then I guess all's well that ends well." I flop onto a chair.

"By the way, Mary asked to hitch a ride back to LA with us."

"Oh!" I perk up. "She wouldn't do that if she were still upset with me—or Evan, for that matter."

Jack winces. "Don't be surprised if she still gives you the silent treatment. She finds going back with us less disgusting than boarding a flight with Chad, no matter how hard Mario is begging her to stick it out in Washington. Apparently, she was successful in passing along some intel."

"She must have been the one who snuffed out that Yelena was working with another mole." My heart swells with pride. "I guess the best thing that came out of this mission is that she's finally had her fill of diplomatic intelligence."

Jack looks me in the eye. "Despite knowing she's got great instincts, do you still feel she's not cut out for it?"

"I just want her to have a normal life!" Anxious now, I move to the window and look out. "To go to college, have a blast with old and new friends, enjoy her classes; to learn things about the world that aren't dark and sinister. To travel. You know—like normal people."

"What we want for her won't matter," he insists. "Only what she wants for herself counts."

"Yes, I know that. I just…want her…to respect me again." I lower my head. "And Evan. She hasn't given him a chance to explain what he did with Yelena and why."

Jack pulls me onto the bed beside him. "I think you've got it wrong. She hasn't lost her respect for you. Mary knows you hate the honeypot part of the job. And she sees now firsthand how dangerous our job is. She worries about you—about us. She just wants for us what we want for her: normalcy."

"Will we ever have that? I mean, will we ever be free to be ignorant of the world we know?"

"Whoever said 'ignorance is bliss' was right." Jack cradles my head. "At some point, everyone steps away from the game. When that day comes for us, I'll welcome it."

"Me too," I whisper.

A thought comes to me: Has anyone told Mary that Crystal isn't all so innocent?"

"Nope. Mario, Marcus, and I agreed we'd leave that honor to you. It'll be the perfect icebreaker on the flight home."

"If you insist." I hope he's right.

WITHIN FIFTEEN MINUTES, AIR FORCE ONE IS WHEELS UP.

I look out my window to see it fly off. In the driveway, Crystal does the same.

When she sees me, I wave.

'Til we meet again, bitch.

She flips me a bird, so I assume she has no desire for a reunion.

I join Lee, Jack, Marcus, and Mario on the front porch. The conversation is about sports: a Dodgers game against San Francisco in a few days. Mario and Marcus will hang out here at Lee's dude ranch and then tag along to enjoy his box seats.

"Hey, why don't we take the kids too?" Jack suggests.

"Sure. They'll enjoy that," Lee replies.

I stifle the urge to box my ears to test that I heard right: my sweet husband and dear friend have made peace.

Just then, we hear police car sirens—

And then we see an ambulance.

Lee grabs a pair of binoculars and searches the ribbon of highway that follows the vast plain to the horizon. "I see the problem. There's a wreck a couple of miles down the road."

Soon, two more ambulances are screaming down the blacktop, and three more police cars.

Twenty minutes later, one of the police cars heads our way.

Mary, Evan, Abu, and Arnie are now on the porch.

As the officer exits the car, Lee heads out to meet him. What he hears has him beckoning us over.

When we get there, Lee tells the policeman to repeat the information:

This is how we learn that Crystal's car crashed into a tree—

But that she was already dead—

—From asphyxiation;

When they opened the door, they caught a whiff of something that smelled like rotting fruit. A couple of them gagged from it. They're being checked out by the paramedics now.

It was nerve gas.

"We had to mask up to get out the woman's body. She had this in her hand." The officer holds up a satellite phone:

The remote control.

"We found its source in her trunk—a statue of some sort. There was a canister in a drawer in its base."

Horrified, Mary gasps. She puts her hand over her mouth and runs out into the yard. She only gets a few feet away before she starts vomiting.

Evan goes after her. When he gets to her side, he holds her head. He waits until she signals she can walk again and then takes her back to the couch on the porch. I follow. When I reach Mary, Evan gets up so that I may sit with her. As she curls up in my arms, she gasps, "Poor Crystal."

"No, Mary!" Mario insists. "'Poor Crystal' was a Russian mole. She was working in tandem with Lara Owensby, another Russian asset. I specifically had you placed in Senator Bennington's staff because we suspected an intelligence leak was coming from there. We just didn't know from whom."

Mary's eyes grow wide. "You mean that Lee's girl-friend was…." She winces as her eyes seek him out.

He shrugs.

At least Jack has the decency to turn his head so that Lee doesn't see his smirk.

Marcus insists, "Mary, your mother's instincts about Crystal were right. But the question is, how did she gas herself as opposed to everyone on Air Force One?"

Teary-eyed, Mary admits, "I switched the statues. I'd noticed that the base on the one that was given to POTUS had a nick on it, so I took it upon myself to replace the statue with the one that was to go to Omaha with the Benningtons—well, that is, Mrs. Bennington. Since the statues are identical, I didn't think anyone would notice, let alone mind." Mary bows her head. "I…I guess I inadvertently killed Crystal."

"You also saved the lives of everyone aboard Air Force One," Mario reminds her.

Mary frowns. "With all due respect, sir: why didn't you let me in on the Bennington intel when I accepted your offer?"

Her bluntness stuns Mario for a long moment. Finally: "Had I told you, and for some reason, you'd been asked point blank by either of the Benningtons, you may have given yourself away."

"You kept me informed on that social media cruise junket on the last mission, and I did everything you asked of me," Mary retorts. "Wasn't that proof enough that I could keep my mouth shut under pressure?"

Mario slaps his forehead. "Jeez, no respect for authority! Like mother, like daughter."

"Nothing wrong with that!" Mary and I say in unison.

"Okay, yeah. Keep telling yourself that." He sighs. "There's also a little thing called 'plausible deniability.' As an NSA asset, everything you do must be by the book—unlike your parents' antics."

"Excuse me?" I retort. "Her 'parents' antics' have pulled your fat out of the fire on many occasions."

"Mario, have you forgotten that I was supposed to be on that plane too? Had I not made the switch, I would be dead now, along with everyone else who got onboard." Mary points out.

"We suspected it was in the statue and searched it before take-off, along with everyone's luggage," Abu tells her. "That's how we knew it wasn't onboard. We just assumed that our intel about a sabotage attempt had been wrong, as was Donna's guess regarding the statue."

Mary turns to me. "You guessed the killing device was hidden there?"

When I nod, she stares incredulously at me. But then, to Mario, she declares: "Bottom line: if you're going to keep me out of the loop, I see no need to complete my internship with you."

"Hallelujah!" Evan mutters. "I told you you'd be better off at BlackTech."

"No one said I'll be interning with your firm either," Mary declares. "We still have a lot to discuss." Mary's gaze shifts to me. "In fact, you and I also need to talk—"

A cell phone buzzes.

It's the burner phone in which Crystal's actual SIM card has been placed.

The text that's come in reads:

Swan sang last song. Fly home, Azrael.
SEA ☮ (47 °16′ 03′N 122 ° 8′ 27 °W)
—Bull

"'Bychkov' is the Russian word for 'bull!'" Arnie crows triumphantly. "The toddler Russian-language flash cards paid off!"

"Which means that Stepan somehow knows Yelena is dead," I reason.

"It also means that 'Crystal' is now confirmed as Azrael," Marcus says. "Yelena must be 'swan,' which is 'Levedeva' in Russian."

Arnie claps slowly. "Masterful deduction, sir!"

Abu nudges him. "Not only does he run the whole US Intelligence Community, he knows Russian without your stupid little flash cards. Go figure."

Arnie's face turns red.

"I guess now that we have our adversaries' true surnames, between that and facial recognition analysis their real identities should pop up on Acme's database," Jack deduces. "Not that it matters since two of them are dead."

"Could SEA mean Seattle?" I ask. "is that where he expects to rendezvous with her?"

"My guess is yes," Marcus replies. "We'll have confirmation by pulling up the location at that latitude and longitude."

"The answer regarding Seattle is affirmative," Emma reports. "It's the Westin Seattle."

"If she's going back to Russia, it's certainly the closest port of call," Mario reasons. He slaps me on the back. "Welcome back to the living, Crystal."

19

When Guests Overstay Their Welcome

IT'S HAPPENED IN THE PAST:

A few of your party's guests linger after everyone else is gone.

They've made themselves comfortable in a cozy corner of your living room (or out by your pool or fire pit) and seem to have settled in for the night.

When a few gentle hints—pointedly staring at your watch; loud goodbyes to others; yawning in the lingerers' faces—doesn't seem to move them, try the following:

Tip #1: Call the cops about a disturbance—at your address.

You can do it one of two ways. Perhaps borrow your neighbor's phone and pretend you are her complaining over the "seemingly endless party next door;" or call from your phone and claim you have a home invasion. Either way, the cops will come in guns blazing, and your guests will take the hint that it's time to skedaddle.

Tip #2: Shoot off your cannon.

No need to save it for Memorial Day, Independence Day, and various and sundry military parades. Before you can say, "Forward the Light Brigade!..." the malingerers will be gone. Well-known fact: people run faster when they think they're under attack.

What…you say you don't have a cannon? Trust me, it's an excellent investment! Not only will the sound scare the bejesus out of them, but it'll also send a clear message: that overstaying your welcome will cost you dearly, like, say, your hearing, for at least a week.

Tip #3: Release the hounds.

It's why you have them, right? You'll also see how fast your so-called friends can run when chased by ferocious beasts who haven't been fed for a few days.

MARY FOLLOWS THROUGH ON HER DECISION TO COME HOME.

Which means she must first fly with us to Seattle.

Despite allowing me to comfort her after learning of Crystal's death, now her interaction with me is polite but distant.

Maybe it's for the best. I need to be focused on the extermination of Stepan. Whereas it's to be an officially unsanctioned hit, the order comes from above. While carrying out an assassination attempt on POTUS, Stepan swung for the fences and missed.

As Crystal, I can't miss either.

And I won't.

Mary's coolness extends to Evan. Because I feel this is my fault for having unwittingly divulged his indiscretion, I ask him to follow me into the bedroom suite of the plane so that I may apologize.

He accepts my mea culpa with a shrug. "I get it. You'd thought I'd followed through and had already told Mary. I should have, but we were both so happy to see each other and to learn how her mission and mine had somehow converged that we never got around to it."

"Then you don't hate me for letting the cat out of the bag?"

Evan shakes his head. "The only thing I hate is that Mary still hasn't given me a chance to explain what happened and why."

"Would you like me to call her in now and leave the two of you alone?"

"You wouldn't mind?"

"Not at all."

I go over to Mary, who's reading a magazine. "Evan has something to discuss with you. He's in the bedroom."

"I'm not interested in anything he has to say," she mutters.

"Don't you want to talk things out?" I ask.

"I think I have a very clear picture of what happened. If I change my mind, I know where to find him—and you, too, for that matter."

"At least tell him that."

"You need to butt out of this," Mary says firmly.

We don't talk for the rest of the flight.

CRYSTAL'S RENDEZVOUS IS TO HAPPEN AT THE FOUR SEASONS Seattle.

I get no more texts from Stepan until I'm across the street from the sixty-story hotel. He must have eyes on me because, at that point, I'm texted the name under which the room has been reserved: Annabelle Nightingale. Both names are English iterations of what Acme now knows as Crystal's real name: Anya Solovyova. The only picture Acme found of her shows her as a brunette instead of Crystal's ash blond hair.

With a bit of a trim, my own brown hair will do.

Acme assumes Stepan doesn't yet know of Crystal's untimely demise. But we've no doubt that he's quite aware of Crystal's failure to murder POTUS and the rest of the passengers on Air Force One while it was mid-air, which has him understandably wary.

At the front desk, I'm handed a room card and told to catch the express elevator to the eighteenth floor. With my lenses and mics in place, Acme knows this as well.

Jack and Abu are shadowing me, but the best they can do is to hope that at least one, if not both, of the rooms on either side of Stepan's suite, are vacant so that they can secure those too.

I've just tapped the lock with the key card when the door opens. Stepan has expensive taste: the suite, modern and sumptuous, overlooks Elliott Bay and the necklace of islands beyond it—

Not that I can do more than glance at it. Immediately,

I'm enveloped in Stepan's arms. Ferociously, his lips devour mine. When we part, he murmurs: "*Ya skuchal po tebe, dorogaya zhena!*"

"Shite!" Emma whispers into my ear. "He called Anya his 'dear wife!'"

I gasp.

Shite is right…

Stepan takes my response as tacit approval to start undressing me.

I back off. "I…I'm sorry about the mission."

He sighs. Then: "*Kak eto sluchilos'?*"

"He's asking how it happened," Emma murmurs.

"Apparently, someone noticed that the statue given to the president had a scratch on the base and changed it out for the other. I didn't find out until after the switch had been made."

He blinks but says nothing. Does he doubt I'm telling the truth?

"*Gde seychas drugaya statuya?*" I may not know what he's saying, but I hear the change in his tone: harder, darker.

I shrug while Emma whispers: "'Where is the other statue now?' Say it in Russian, this way: "*YA zaryl yego v pustyne.*"

Ah, hell.

With great deliberation, I reply: "*YA…ya yel.. yego v pustyne.*"

He stares as if seeing me for the very first time.

He sighs and tosses his arms up, resigned to this reality—

Then slaps me so hard that I'm sent reeling. I slam against the wall.

Stepan doesn't wait for me to catch my balance. He grabs me by my hair and propels me against another wall.

The force stuns me. I sink to the floor.

I'm too shocked to move as he pulls my hair to one side. Stepan sees it: the tiny earpiece:

My lifeline.

Stepan rips it from my ear, walks to the terrace, and throws it into the great beyond.

I scramble to my feet and run to the door—

But he tackles me, crushing me against the plush, suffocating carpet. I manage to turn my head to one side. Stepan puts his face next to mine, looks me in the eye, and chuckles. "I'm going to pluck out your eyes so your friends can no longer see me through those lenses."

I shut my eyes tightly. With his knee on my back and my arms wrenched behind me, I can't break his grip.

Stepan laughs. It takes a moment, but the next thing I know, he's wrapped something—his tie, perhaps—around my eyes.

Then, in English, he growls: "When we get to Moscow, you're going to regret having tried to replace her."

"I'm not going to Moscow, Stepan, and neither are you. It's game over."

He roars with laughter. "Have you forgotten that I have diplomatic immunity? I've put it to good use in situations that make this look like child's play. A whore spy sent to entrap me? If your handlers try pulling that card, believe me, they'll let me go so quickly that you'll be spinning in your grave—if there's enough of you to even bury."

He rises. A second later, so do I because he's twisting my arm as he jerks me forward and drags me over to something—the room's desk, I suppose. The force of his arm against my spine holds me there until he maneuvers something out of a drawer:

The prick of the needle is swift.

I black out.

I HEAR SCREAMING.

The voice, wracked with pain and spewing curses, is mine.

Another voice—Stepan's—promises that the cigarette searing a hole in my back will be the first of many in retribution for Anya's disappearance.

I shrug. "Where am I?" This is a shot in the dark. I've been out for who knows how long, and I'm still blind-folded. And yet, I get the feeling that I'm no longer in the hotel.

Is that why Jack hasn't rescued me? Is it because he doesn't know where I am?

As if reading my mind, Stepan declares, "If you're expecting company, I'm sorry to disappoint you. Your handlers may know where you went—even the exact suite —but we left a different way."

My heart seems to crack into tiny little pieces. Harshly, I vow: "They will find me."

His laugh reverberates through the room. "If you say so." He leans in so close that I feel the heat of his breath: "Where is she? If you're worth something, they may consider a trade."

He thinks she's still alive.

It's my turn to smirk. "I'm worth twice your bigamist wife, so yes, they will." I brace myself for the feel of his cigarette on my skin…

For the smell of burning flesh.

Instead, he punches me in the gut.

I double over.

When I finally catch my breath again and straighten up, he blows his cigarette smoke in my face. Ignoring my coughs, he says, "I'll need a contact number—and your real name."

As best as I can, I croak out the number of a secure Acme phone line that switches to a different feed within seconds of the call's transfer to Ryan and then disconnects so that it's untraceable. "Tell them Donna Stone Craig is your guest."

The silence is a full minute before the room shakes with laughter. "Ah, I'm hosting the infamous American honeypot who stole Putin's NFL Super Bowl ring right off his finger!"

"Let's be real: Vlad stole it first—from its rightful owner, the Patriot team's Robert Kraft."

"Our great leader insists it was a gift!" Stepan retorts. "You Americans always have a way of twisting reality." He sighs. "Too bad you're not worth more than Anya."

"Who says I'm not?" I huff.

"You may be right. Putin may want you in Moscow to atone for your thievery." He tweaks my nose. "You know, in my country, the crime for theft can be as much as two years of 'corrective labor.' Having stolen from Putin, you may be in for a life sentence."

"If you take me with you, believe me: you won't get your wife back. She'll immediately go into our prison system." I click my tongue. "She wouldn't last a week there."

"Who says she won't be going to Moscow as well? You underestimate me, Mrs. Craig." Stepan chuckles. "I'll bet you didn't know I once had a run-in with your current husband, Jack Craig. He'd turned one of our assets. When the woman explained how inspired she was by him, not only was I in charge of her torture, I lobbied to exterminate him as well. Ironically, your husband at the time, Carl Stone, insisted that keeping Jack in play was part of the Quorum's bigger picture, so your beloved dodged a bullet." Stepan's voice is closer now. "I hear Carl's jealousy of Mr. Craig was why he lost his edge—and his life, at your doing."

"I suppose he loved me in his own way," I concede. "But not enough to stay true to our country." Gently, I add: "You must love Anya very much to save me for her trade."

He's silent for so long that I wonder if he's left the room. Finally: "I am nothing without her."

"How did you meet?"

"Directorate S—The SVR's spy school—recruited us while we were at university. We were already in love and diligent students. I'm sure that is why our professors passed our names forward to the SVR."

"What were you studying?" I ask.

"Anya's specialty was languages, whereas I was a history major: thoroughly enthralled with Russia's romantic past: from its Imperial roots to its stoic adherence to the Communist doctrine at all costs—anything to beat back you Capitalist barbarians."

"You've read *War and Peace* too many times," I mutter.

My sass earns me a hard slap.

"You're too flippant for your own good, Mrs. Craig. Now, excuse me while I make the call that saves your life."

I'm only safe as long as he doesn't find out that Anya is dead.

I say prayers that when the call is routed to Ryan, he'll know by what Stepan says that I've allowed him to think that Anya is still alive and will play along.

The wait seems interminable.

In time, I hear Stepan's footsteps.

"In three hours, the exchange takes place at the airport," he says.

"I assume I'm to stay blindfolded until then."

"You assume correctly."

"Can you at least lead me to the powder room?"

"Only if you don't mind company," Stepan replies.

I shake my head. "I'll hold my water."

"Suit yourself."

Silence.

"Continue, Scheherazade," I insist.

"Why are you so interested in my wife and me?" The question comes out gruffly.

"Because, like Jack with me, you'll do anything to protect her," I answer softly. "And I'm a sucker for a good love story."

I wait silently for too long. Finally, he continues: "You know the drill. Those who Directorate S train to be 'illegals' are given names of American or Canadian children who died a few days after birth. After obliterating any record of the death certificate, it recreates the child's identity. We memorize each imaginary detail: where we went to school, our friends and pets, and the teachers who motivated or tortured us. Drivers' licenses and passports are authentic albeit forged."

"What you call an 'iron legend,'" I respond.

"Exactly. The only thing real in our lives is our allegiance to our country and to each other; the passion and the love we share."

"You've always had each other's backs."

"It is the same with you and Jack," he concedes.

"It has to be. Without trust, what we share—the intel we have—is in jeopardy, as are our lives."

Stepan grunts in agreement.

"How did Anya meet Chad?" I ask.

They were both Congressional aides at the time. He's got that good ol' boy charisma that does well in his state. She wrapped him around her finger and then inspired him to greater heights. The rest is history."

"Directorate S must have been tickled pink with this turn of events."

"Of course! What foreign adversary wouldn't be ecstatic to have such an ignorant idiot as an unwitting asset!" Again, he blows smoke in my face. "We could have run him all the way to the White House if it hadn't been for you—or Anya in his place as the grieving Congressional widow." He guffaws. "Your political parties are just as keen to play puppet master."

"I'm sure that Russia would have reveled in a repeat of President Bradley Edmonton's treason," I retort. "Ah, well, too bad. You know what they say: fool the US once, shame on you. Fool it twice, shame on us." During Mission Horoscope, Acme discovered that, while in college, Edmonton, an American citizen, was also turned into a Russian asset.

"Don't forget Babette Chiffray," Stepan adds. "Though she was a Quorum operative, a lot of her intel found its way into our hands."

"The Quorum's intel always went to the highest bidder." Snickering, I add: "Sadly, I don't think I'll ever forget that bitch."

"I hope I've satisfied your curiosity about my little love story, Mrs. Craig." I hear him stand up. "Does it strike you that, in many ways, our lives are mirror images?"

"I suppose you're right—we're doppelgängers. It's why Jack is now compelled to come to my rescue, just as you're doing for Anya. Afterward, we shall both be on our merry way."

Stepan says nothing.

I don't like that.

THOUGH IT MAY SEEM LIKE A MILLION YEARS WHEN YOU'RE sitting in a room blindfolded with no human contact, I know it's been much less—not even two hours—when Stepan announces, "We'll leave now in case Acme has planned any surprises."

He yanks me to my feet and shoves me in front of him.

When we stop, the whisper of air on my face and his nudge to take a step forward are the only hints that I'm entering an elevator. By its gravitational pull, I can tell we are going down.

Silently I count the seconds until it opens again. I'm hit with a hot blast of air. Our footsteps reverberate on the concrete.

We're in a public garage.

I'm steered to the left for a few steps and then to the right for many more. In time, Stepan stops.

I hear the click of a car door. "Get in," Stepan says.

I do as I'm told.

He sits beside me, which means another Russian asset is driving. Perhaps another is riding shotgun. If they talk, I'll know for sure.

I realize we're in a limousine when he taps the glass between him and the driver. He says something in Russian that ends with "…SeaTac tarmac.." The glass muffles the driver's simple response: "Da."

Within twenty minutes, the car comes to a stop.

We sit tight. Stepan says nothing to me.

An hour later, Stepan says, "Your people have arrived, Mrs. Craig."

"And Anya?" I try to keep the dread out of my voice.

He unties my blindfold so that I can see for myself.

Yes, I see her: like me, she sits in the backseat of a dark sedan on the side that faces us. Evan is driving.

Jack sits in the back seat with her.

She, too, is brunette now that she is no longer Crystal Bennington but Anya Solovyova.

Mary would know that. She would also know Anya's inflections and her stride.

Mary is Anya.

I look down.. I can't give away the anxiety I feel about my daughter having to take on the role that would save me.

What is happening?

Her car is on one side of the plane, which I assume will whisk Stepan and so-called Anya away. Ours is on the other.

"You're to step out and walk with me. Very slowly, we will move toward the plane. Anya and Mr. Craig will do the same. We will meet in the middle. You will walk off with Mr. Craig, and my wife will go with me."

I nod.

Stepan opens the door and gets out. He then gives me his hand.

As I step out of the car, He places his other hand on my shoulder.

I feel a prick.

"Did you..." I can't say anymore. My throat is closing up.

He walks me forward.

WE TAKE SLOW, DELIBERATE STEPS TOWARD JACK AND so-called Anya.

My tongue doesn't work. It's as if watching a movie in slow motion:

Smiling triumphantly, the Anya clone suddenly quickens her pace.

At first, Jack tries to keep up with her, but she's moving so quickly that he can't.

When she reaches us, she only has eyes for Stepan. Her head turns up to his.

He yields to his instinct to kiss her.

As they do, she turns him slightly, clinching him in a tight hug—

Stepan gasps. A spasm roils his body.

He sags onto Mary.

She shrugs him off, but she's trembling.

By now, my view of this is a spiraling tilt-a-whirl in which Mary's face looms large. Her eyes are now opened wide with horror. She puts her arms around me and holds tight, as if she'll never let me go.

20

Thank-You Notes

AFTER YOU'VE ATTENDED AN EVENT, A SINCERE NOTE OF thanks is always appreciated by your hostess. It should include the following:

1: A touching salutation. *Make it personal and heartfelt. (Tip: should your feelings lean toward the negative, do your best to tamp down the urge to write: "Yo, Bitch…")*

2: A personal observation. *Your hostess worked incredibly hard to make the day special. Pointing out some minor detail that has caught your eye shows you've paid attention! (And it may pay off in cash if you're willing to keep secret her covert kiss in the hallway with her best friend's hubby.)*

3: Some form of reciprocation. *It doesn't need to be a whole party in your hostess's honor. It could be something as simple as a chocolate cake with a thank-you card—although I'm sure she'd appreciate your promise to never poison her dog again, no matter how often it does its business in your yard.*

(Tip: making the cake from her dog's mess should also make your point.)

❧

WHEN I AWAKE, I'M IN THE BEDROOM I'VE COME TO KNOW almost as well as my own: the one on Acme's plane.

Mary is sitting beside me. When she realizes my eyes are open, she leaps to kiss me. Next, she's out the door to exclaim: "Mom has finally come around!"

Jack is the first to come in, but Evan, Abu, and Arnie are on his heels. Though I try to sit up, Jack shakes his head. "Take it easy, Don."

I nod. Then I take a deep breath. "Works for me. So, tell me the full story from the beginning."

"Only the bottom ten floors of the building make up the hotel," Jack explains. "However, the top ten floors are condominiums, which use a different elevator and garage. Stepan's hotel suite was on the tenth floor. The CIA has always suspected that this particular hotel suite has been permanently leased by the SVR. It has known for years that right above it is a condominium owned by a Russian oligarch and is used as an SVR safe house. Acme deduced that there is some sort of opening between the two units."

"How did Acme discover its deduction was correct?" I ask.

"Besides watching the traffic in the halls and elevators, we also kept an eye on both garages. Stepan made no movement from either for three hours. Our hunch played out when he contacted Ryan with the offer to swap you for

Anya. Two hours later, he exited via the condominium's garage."

"I was worried that Ryan would unwittingly divulge Anya's death during Stepan's call," I explain.

"To Stepan's detriment, he wrongly assumed that we'd detained her and were using her as a bargaining chip," Jack replies. "Frankly, had Stepan suspected the worst-case scenario—that her death was even a possibility—he may have led with that."

"More than likely, he would have killed me the minute he realized I wasn't Anya." I frown. "I guess I botched my Russian phrasing."

Abu nods. "You said, 'I ate it in the desert' instead of 'I buried it in the desert.'"

"Yikes! No wonder he tortured me." I look over at Jack. "When we got out of the car during the hostage exchange, Stepan pricked me with something. My guess is that he was pulling Yelena's trick: hoping I'd have a heart attack while he and Anya flew off into the wild blue yonder. The stunt would have protected his diplomatic immunity."

"We anticipated he might try some form of payback for ruining their mission and came prepared with Digibind," Jack says. "Two can play that game. When Mary went in for a kiss with him, she pricked his heart with a Digitalis dart. Officially he died of a pulmonary embolism."

"Talk about poetic justice! A broken heart—or in this case, a heart attack." I flinch as I shift so I'm not pressing on my burns.

Mary takes my hand. "I saw the cigarette marks on

your back. I'm so sorry, Mom, that you had to endure Stepan's torture."

I tear up. "I knew what I signed up for." Seeing the pain on her face, I assume she wants me to leave it at that. Fine. Not that I'll change the subject to something less painful: "Mary, are you talking to Evan again?"

Mary nods. "He explained that he knew he could have... that Yelena offered herself up to him. Instead, he beat her up." Her tears fall freely. "She reminded him of his mother: when you're the enemy, sex, pain, and death are transactional. Yelena could have just as easily killed him as seduced him."

"In other words, they are like me." There, I've said it.

I'm waiting for her to nod or recoil, repulsed. Instead, she adamantly shakes her head. "You're wrong, Mom. You're nothing like them! Catherine was in it for the money and the power. She was willing to trade state secrets for it. Yelena did great harm to our country and killed indiscriminately. You do it for *us:* your family, your country." Mary takes my hand. "I was a fool to give you grief over what you must do in your job. You are the strongest woman I know! I saw how you prove it by shutting off that part of your mind while you subjugate yourself to the will of others if it gets you to your goal: taking them down."

"I'm not always happy with how I get the job done," I admit. "Still, I've learned to accept that the means justify the end. Thank you for acknowledging it too." My eyes find hers. "My dear sweet Mary, you saved my life. But you don't have to feel you need to keep doing it! Ours is not a family business. We're not doctors, lawyers, dentists, or shopkeepers. Honestly, I wish you'd had a normal summer before starting college."

Mary's eyes bore into mine. "If that was what I'd wanted, I wouldn't have gone off into the woods with you to learn survival skills. And I wouldn't have accepted Mario's offer to work with him—especially when the job entailed keeping an eye on that creep, Chad Bennington." She shivers at the thought. "Remember, our mutual goal this summer was to see if I had it in me to continue on this course. What I learned is that I have good instincts for this profession. But I also saw its dark side: how it eats away at your innocence, at your desire to trust others. I projected my horror at the reality of this profession onto you. I was wrong to do that." Mary bows her head. "I'm glad you can forgive me for that bit of stupidity."

"Disgust for what we see in the field is a natural instinct," I insist.

"So was my drive to protect you when I knew you were in danger—just as I'd do the same for Dad and Evan—and the rest of the Acme team. I've come to realize each of you has the same desire: protect and defend: your loved ones, of course, but your country too." Mary's hand moves to my cheek. "I can do that best by having your back. And I know you'll have mine too." She smiles. "And when the time is right, we'll walk away from this life knowing we did a lot of good in the world. And we'll rejoice that we've survived."

"If this is the life you want, so be it." I can't keep the sobs out of my voice.

Now Mary is crying too. And she's hugging me.

In time we untangle ourselves, but our emotions are still frayed. Otherwise, why would I be laughing hysterically and crying just as riotously?

Over the plane's intercom, George announces: "If you look out on the left side of the plane, you'll see the bright lights of Los Angeles. Welcome home, my Acme teammates."

Finally.

Tomorrow Aunt Phyllis, Jeff, and Trisha will be home too—

And I'll be immersed in the frenzy and joy that comes with attending the wedding of your dearest friend.

In my case, it's my aunt, Phyllis.

"I thought I knew you. Boy, was I wrong." I'm in our backyard hammock with Aunt Phyllis.

"Are you talking about the fact that one of my feet only has four toes?" She raises a leg—easy enough to do since it's almost *in* my face and visa-versa.

You bet I stare at it to ensure she isn't just playing with me.

But, of course, she is.

As punishment, I tickle her foot. Giggling, she jerks it back, making the hammock rock precariously. I realize this is stupid since I'm still hung over from last night's bachelorette party in her honor. I take a few deep breaths to quell the urge to vomit, then mutter, "No, silly! I meant I didn't realize how many interesting people you know."

Phyllis's giggles roll into snorts. "I do have a life outside the Family Formerly Known as Stone. In those numerous decades that I've yet to admit to, I've collected quite a clown car of questionable characters who are there for me at a moment's notice. Not all are anarchists, hippies, and reprobates, mind you."

"I was honored to meet some of them last night." Aunt Phyllis must hear the sincerity in my voice because she reaches out for my hand and pats it. "Like that woman who had previously been a district court justice—"

"And also one of the anarchists in my life." My aunt sighs. "Ah, good times! You should see how quickly she can mix up a Molotov cocktail!"

"And then there's the lady who started a tech firm, built it into a multimillion-dollar conglomerate, sold it, and gave all the money away to charity—"

"She's a hoot, isn't she? Who knew she was the only one who could do four somersaults on the bar without falling off? As one of the first people to invest in her firm when it went public, you'll never have to worry about the kids' college educations. It's my gift to you and to them. Heaven knows that slave master of yours, Ryan, pays you a pittance for all you do on his behalf." Phyllis rolls her eyes.

No arguments there.

"How about that lady who kept tipping the Chippendales dancers to pull you up on the stage? What's her story?" I ask.

"Nobel Prize winner. Rarely gets out in public. Now you know why." Aunt Phyllis sighs. "I thank the Lord I was gifted with nerves of steel, a bodacious bod, and the determination to live my life to the fullest. It's why I attract good folks."

"I wish I'd followed your example on that last blessing."

"You are everything I am, plus so much more." My aunt's voice is soft but firm. "Your mother would have been so proud of you."

"I can only hope so," I whisper. "Albeit, sometimes I wonder if Mother would have approved of how I've lived my life, both as a professional and as a mother."

"Sweet, sweet Donna!" Phyllis's eyes drill into mine. "Don't ever doubt that she would have been right beside you—that she *is* right beside you in her own way— cheering you on."

I nod resignedly—and then ask because I've always wondered: "Okay, level with me: you do know what I do, right?"

My aunt's smile fades. "Even before you started working with Acme, I knew you'd end up there. Jack gave it away."

"*Jack*?... When? How?"

"After Carl left you. I found Jack snooping around my garage, looking for clues about Carl. At the time, I didn't know why. Then again, I always felt there was something fishy about Carl. He was too dark and too mysterious— and not in a good way." She shrugs. "I figured if this stranger needed help proving Carl had wronged you, I was all for that."

"All these years...I never knew!... So, how did you figure out that Jack was one of the good guys?"

"Honey, other than watching agog as I threw down a few dirty dancing moves that had even the Chippendales boys' eyes popping out of their heads, didn't you learn anything new last night about your dear Aunt Phyllis?"

"Um...you mean other than the fact you hang with some fascinating people?"

Taking one look at my stymied face, she sighs and leans in and whispers: "It's easy to fool others when they don't take you seriously. Most 'dumb blondes' are actually pretty smart cookies. The guy who's always snipping away at his hedges with clippers sees everything that happens on his street. Secretaries usually know more than their bosses. No matter what their parents tell them in sugar-sweet voices, little kids know exactly what their parents are really thinking just by reading their faces. And although older folk are ignored, they see and hear everything."

I bow to her. "I'll never underestimate another human being again—least of all you."

Phyllis nods. "Everyone has a piece of the puzzle. If you know how to ask, they'll share it with you too." She rolls out of the hammock. "We better get a move on. You've still got to shoe-horn me into my wedding dress!"

TO MY MIND, AUNT PHYLLIS IS ALWAYS BEAUTIFUL.

Today, she is stunning. Her blush-tone jewel-neck floor-length capelet gown shimmers with turquoise, orange, green, yellow and purple iridescent embroidery. With her arms at her side, her sleeves, like sheer bat wings, are as long as her dress.

Aunt Phyllis' "something old" is her mother's long white leather gloves, which my mother also wore on her wedding day, and so did I.

Her "something new" is a lace garter that Trisha bought for her at a wedding shop.

Her "something blue" is a pair of cowboy boots she found at the country store near Lee's ranch.

My aunt's "something borrowed" is the locket that has been my keepsake, given to me by my mother. Jack once called it our good luck charm. At the time, we didn't know Carl had secreted a microdot containing the access code to Acme's agent directory on the picture I kept of him there.

It now holds a picture of our family: Jack, the kids, Aunt Phyllis and me. Today, we'll take a new photo that will include Porter.

The estate's beautiful garden, overlooking the Pacific Ocean, is a fantastic venue for the sunset ceremony. It's a packed house. Porter's family has come from every corner of the country. Like him, they are kind and rock-solid with purpose. They share his deep chuckle and his sly sense of humor.

The procession begins with the officiant taking his place: in this case, Ryan, who was ordained for the occasion. Being part of Porter's weekly poker game has earned him this honor.

The groom is accompanied by his best man: Marcus,

who trained Porter when he first came under his department at the NSA.

As Aunt Phyllis's Matron of Honor, Jody chose a beautiful dress for me: a body-skimming one-shoulder sheath that looks as if it's been spattered in turquoise, green, deep purple, and yellow paint. Marcus's bowtie has all of these colors.

I'm preceded by Phyllis' other bridesmaids. Their dresses are the same cut as mine, except each is in just one of its colors. Mary's is yellow. Trisha's is green. Janie's is pink. Jody's dress is turquoise, and Eve has purple. Our bouquets are a riot of these colors.

The bowties worn by Porter's groomsmen mirror one of these colors too. Jack's matches Trisha's, as does Evan's to Mary's. Jeff's matches Janie's. Dominic—who walks wincingly with a cane—wears one that matches Jody's dress. Lee's bowtie mirrors Eve's purple dress.

Harrison and Nicky are the ring bearers.

Ryan's marriage blessing is the right combination of humor, inspiration, and joyous good wishes. Be it to laughter or tears or both, everyone is moved.

As Ryan proclaims that it's time to kiss the bride, Porter leans Phyllis all the way back. When their lips meet, the cheers reach a frenzied crescendo.

Finally, they part. Porter shouts, "Let the party begin!"

By hook or by crook, Jody somehow booked Trevor Hall's band: deep melodies, great lyrics, smooth segues, and enough highs to keep everyone dance-happy.

Jeff slowly dances with Janie's head on his shoulder. Lee stops to watch. Is he awed by this waypoint in the quick march of time? Perhaps he's savoring one of these all-too-brief moments of parental peace when you know your child is happy, healthy, and safely out of harm's way. Neither Janie nor Harrison are Lee's by blood. No matter. His love, care, and commitment are boundless.

Lee has so much love to give.

He shouldn't waste it on me.

Eve goes to his side. As he stares off absently, she straightens his bowtie.

Looking down, Lee's eyes sweep over her.

I can't make out what she's saying but it makes him laugh—

Ah! I recognize that look: when another's concern is appreciated;

When suddenly you see a person for the very first time.

I know that grin on Lee's face: It says *I adore you too.*

"Finally!" I murmur.

"What is it?" Jack follows my gaze—

He smiles. "Well, I'll be damned! Maybe Lee's crush on you is finally over."

"I can live with that—as long as you'll always be head over heels gaga over me." I lace my fingers behind his neck and pull him close. "You're the one man I cannot live without."

Jack's smile fades as he gets down on one knee. "Donna Shives Stone Craig, will you marry me again?"

I think of the day I first met him: it was hate at first sight.

Slowly, he proved his love: something he'd felt for me even before I knew he was in my life.

Every day may be our last. When the time comes, we've come to understand that we are still intertwined souls for eternity.

I smile down at the man who thrills me like no other.

Then I hold out my hands and pull him back onto his feet.

As Jack picks me up and carries me away, I say, "Sure. Only this time, try not to get kidnapped on our honeymoon. Which reminds me: we never got a refund on that..."

— THE END —

Other Books by Josie Brown

The Extracurricular Series

Books 1, 2, and 3

The Totlandia Series

The Onesies - Book 1 (Fall)

The Onesies - Book 2 (Winter)

The Onesies - Book 3 (Spring)

The Onesies - Book 4 (Summer)

The Twosies - Book 5 (Fall)

The Twosies – Book 6 (Winter)

The Twosies - Book 7 (Spring)

The Twosies - Book 8 (Summer)

The True Hollywood Lies Series

Hollywood Hunk

Hollywood Whore

More Josie Brown Novels

The Candidate

Secret Lives of Husbands and Wives

The Baby Planner

How to Reach Josie

To write Josie, go to:
mailfromjosie@gmail.com

To find out more about Josie, or to get on her eLetter list
for book launch announcements, go to her website:
www.JosieBrown.com

You can also find her at:

www.AuthorProvocateur.com

twitter.com/JosieBrownCA

facebook.com/josiebrownauthor

pinterest.com/josiebrownca

instagram.com/josiebrownnovels